I0603657

Blood Ties Bloody Lies

TJ Ward

Copyrights

National Library of Australia Cataloguing-in Publication Data,
catalogue record for this book is available on request from the
National Library of Australia

ISBN Number: 978-0-6484481-7-4

Acknowledgements

This book has had a long gestation period and after a frustrating exercise in
self-publishing a sci-fi novel, I was fortunate to meet the "two Macs":
Carolyn McAndrew, Publisher with Picardie Press and the introduction to Mentor,
Rochelle McDonnell. Without their advice, insights and feedback it would be just
a story and not the novel it has become.

I also thank Jaqueline Mallard, the late Andrew Mallard's sister for her
contribution to the appendix of the book about her brother's story.
Plus the support of this book by Estelle Blackburn, who I have
great respect for, given her many achievements and personal sacrifice
to be a shining beacon for injustice.

Preface

This story is a fictional novel inspired by the personal experiences of John Button
& Darryl Beamish. Both were accused and convicted of murders they didn't commit
despite the confession by social-outcast Eric Edgar Cooke before he was hanged in
Fremantle prison in Western Australia in 1964.
Other notable cases include Lindy Chamberlain and the late Andrew Mallard.

Foreword

I am an investigative journalist with a passion for pursuing injustice and truth. I agreed to write the foreword to Blood Ties - Bloody Lies because it has a similar theme to my award-winning book Broken Lives.

Broken Lives is about the notorious serial killer who changed the fabric of society in Perth, Western Australia - a city in which, in the early nineteen sixties, people never locked their cars or houses. A once innocent and carefree Perth became frightened, insular and under siege.

My research uncovered many inconsistencies and purposely hidden evidence in two cases - the conviction of John Button for killing his girlfriend by running her down and the conviction of Darryl Beamish for a gruesome axe murder. When finally apprehended, Eric Edgar Cooke confessed to both murders in great detail that only the perpetrator could know. Yet the justice system could not admit its error. *In the Appendix section is a web link to photos of Button and Beamish and their Bio's.*

While Blood Ties - Bloody Lies is a fictional story of secrets and lies, it is a believable account of choosing your friends wisely and how prejudice and injustice impact on those around them. I resonate strongly with the character Kate, the Community Legal Aid lawyer and her actions, as they mirror my journey in uncovering the truth, in my case the wrongful convictions of John and Darryl and malfeasance by both police and judiciary in prosecuting their cases.

Not only is Blood Ties - Bloody Lies a good read, but also a cautionary tale about knowing when to tell the truth and when to speak up before events change beyond the point of no return. It shows how prejudice and injustice can divide a community. Yet when eventually called to account, the community healed those wounds.

I thoroughly recommend the book to you.

Estelle Blackburn

Note: Estelle Blackburn has earnt many awards for her investigative work, notably; the Order of Australia medal, the 2001 Walkley Award for Investigative Journalism, the WA Premier's Book Award and WA Woman of the year for 2005.

Table of Contents

Chapter 1
Birthday Boy

Allow me to introduce myself. My name is Peter Jasper Gannon. I've just turned forty and live on Queensland's Sunshine Coast. Australia is God's own country, eh? I'm a Baker by trade, so the early morning shift allows for afternoons off to indulge in my passion – surfing.

Although I haven't been on planet Earth all that long, I've noticed how events seem to go in cycles. Nature is governed by it: the moon phases, the ebb and flow of the tide, the relentless rhythm of the waves. And for me, today's my birthday. Sadly, my partner Kelly is in Melbourne while her Mum is going through 'Chemo'. However, I've just got a message from Kate Maybury that she's on her way.

I recently bumped into Kate for the third time, while shopping in Brisbane. One wonders about such encounters. Are they truly random or purposeful, synchronous events?

Why do I say that? Kate and I crossed paths some twenty-five years ago under unusual circumstances.

Thirty minutes later there's a knock at the door. A very different Kate from the one I met back then is standing there.

"Hi Kate," I say as I step back and gesture for her to come in. She shakes my hand and says, "I hope I'm not intruding."
"No way," I say. "My cousins Roxy and Josh will be coming over shortly to wish me Happy Birthday, so I wouldn't be on my own."

"Your birthday?" Kate asks with a big grin. "Why didn't you tell me? I would've brought a cake or something. Well, a hug will have to do."

Kate gives me a big hug and says, "I'm almost afraid to ask how old you are."

I hold up four fingers.

When Kate and I first met, she was tall and slim, had short dark hair when 'big hair' was 'in' and was a chain smoker. Since then, she's got herself married, stopped smoking and put on a few kilos. But my most vivid memory is of how smart and confident she was.

I recall the second time we met. It was at the Railway Station in Brisbane. She was pushing a stroller and we went for a coffee to go over old times in Pomona.

I'm brought back to the present on hearing a car pull into the driveway. I hear two car doors slam followed by running steps and a thump on the front door.

Standing at the door are my teen cousins Roxy and Josh jostling with each other to be the first inside. Their Mum, my Aunt Barbara, has dropped them off to help me celebrate.

They're great kids and reckon I'm 'pretty cool' for an 'Oldie'. That's 'cos most of the time I've got a ready answer to their problems.

I usher them in, and Roxy gives me a warm hug; hands me a birthday present, while Josh hangs back.

I tear open the fancy paper and say, "Hey you guys, thanks for dropping in. The t-shirt's dead-set cool. You can never have enough t-shirts. Oh, I should've intro'd you. This is Kate Maybury, who I knew years ago in Pomona. Remember, when Mum and me moved there?"

Kate stands, shaking hands in turn with Roxy and Josh. "I'm pleased to meet you both."

Roxy and Kate sink into the couch. Roxy pulls her legs up and crosses them Buddha fashion, while Josh has my fridge door open eyeing the contents.

"Got any Coke, Big Cuz?" he asks cheekily. "Yeah, down the bottom. What about you two?"
Roxy smiles and nods as I flop down into old favourite, while Kate says, "Just water for me."

I shout to Josh, "Get one for Roxy too and there's a jug of cold water for Kate. I reckon I'll have a can too. Bit warm, eh? Stubbie holders are on top of the fridge."

Roxy is beaming with excitement. She's got news.

"Guess what Pete? I got three gold medals at the interschool sports yesterday!"

"That's fantastic Rox, which events?"

"The 200 Metres, the 4 by 4 Relay and the Long Jump," she gushes.

"Wow, the boys are going to have a hard time catching you." I turn and look at Josh and ask, "What do you reckon, eh Josh?"

He just rolls his eyes while handing me a can. So, I have to ask, "How come your nose is out of joint boy-o? Aren't you proud of your big sister? What's up with you?"

"It's nothin' really," he replies.

"Come on, you can tell me. I know something's wrong, eh?"

Josh thrusts his head towards the couch. "I can't say in front of them."

"Okay," I whisper, "Why don't we go out the front then, and you tell me what's wrong?"

Josh nods and I excuse us both. On our way out the front door, Roxy eyeballs Josh with an intense, suspicious stare.

We both sit on the edge of the front veranda and I ask, "What's troubling you mate?"

Josh bows his head so that he doesn't have to look me in the eye.

"It's like this. School sucks, 'cos I found out Paul, my best mate at school, pinched some money from the canteen. Then, he dobs in this other kid Brian. The trouble is, I know that's wrong, but I can't dob in a mate. Besides, Brian's an arsehole and I reckon he had it coming. He swans around like he owns the place. His Dad's rich and paid for our music room and stuff."

I sit back and look at Josh. "Well, where's the problem?"

Josh leans forward. "The school Principal brought in the cops. Some of the kids are saying if Brian's charged, he'll get a criminal record. If that happens the school's going to lose out big-time. But I just can't dob in my best mate. Is that wrong?"

I lean back, thinking. Where I was brought up, you didn't dare dob. If you did, you'd be labelled a low-life or mongrel dog, yet there are times you have to man up. So I know how Josh feels. I gesture for us to go back inside and usher him through the door.

I close it and put my hand on Josh's shoulder. "I know what you're going through mate, so get comfortable; you too, Roxy. I have an amazing story to tell that greatly affected Kate and me when I was about Roxy's age.

"Josh almost cheers. "Yay! Big Cuz is going to tell us another one of his tall tales."

Roxy giggles and asks, "Did you have the hots for Kate?"

"No way: I was scared of her. Nothing seemed to faze her. When I met her, she'd already been a corporate lawyer in Brisbane in a big firm, a partner, no less, and she was used to working in a man's world."

Kate laughs. "Hang on Roxy, Pete was only fifteen years old back then."

"Well, get settled now. This story is no tall tale. It's one hundred per cent true. And, Josh, it's a story that might help you."

It all happened back in the late Seventies. Yeah, that was a time when I thought life was simpler. Things like 'political correctness' were just two words. Eggs were called fresh. Now they are Battery, Barn Laid, Free-range, Organic and Vegetarian. There was no Internet and 'Google' was something you spread on your toast."

"What sort of spread?" asks Roxy, rocking back and forth on the couch.

"Flavoured peanut paste."

"What flavour, Pete?"

"I think it was either strawberry or vanilla, and the advert used to go: 'here comes Google with his Googly eyes'."

Roxy screws up her face: "Errr, gross!"

"Oh yeah, and flairs and mini shirts were in, and we were Stayin Alive to the disco beat of the Bee Gees.

"As you guys know, my folks had split up by then. My older brother, Jeb, couldn't hack all the hassles and had left months earlier. So it was just Mum and me making the trek up from Melbourne to a small town called Pomona."

"Where's Pomona? I've never heard of it," asks Josh.

"Oh, it's up the coast, about 140 clicks north of Brisbane. Always felt Mum was trying to put as many miles as possible between her and the Old Man."

A car horn interrupts my story, so I get up and look out the window. It's Aunt Barbara, pulling into the drive. I open the front door as she winds down the window and shouts, "I hope my two aren't annoying you, Pete."

Josh gets up and pokes his head out the door. "No Mum, we're not. Pete has just started one of his stories."

She replies, "Well if that's the case, I'll go and do some shopping."

Roxy stretches her arms out and yawns. "Pete, if this story is for Josh, I'll go shopping with Mum."

"Looks like shopping wins. Roxy's coming with you."

Roxy hands me her half-empty can, brushing past me as I hold open the front door. "Happy Birthday, Pete," she says. "Hope you don't mind. I just love shopping! Nice to meet you, Kate."

Kate waves, "Likewise Roxy. I'd choose shopping too."

I close the door and ask, "Okay guys, where was I?

"Oh, before I go on Josh, I want Kate to be aware of what your problem is about, whether it's right or not to 'dob' on your best mate.

Anyway, I'm sure this story will help you to make up your mind.

"I recall the folks in Pomona were shy. They didn't take kindly to new folk, especially an un-hitched, good-looking sort like my Mum. She must've been a threat to the womenfolk.

"Mind you, they had good reason to feel that way. Some of the Hubbies thought Mum was fair game. In such a small town, it only takes a couple of hopeful Romeos to set off the prying eyes and wagging tongues."

Kate nods her head. "Yes, you got that right. I had similar unwanted attention too."

I continue. "They weren't to know that was the last thing on Mum's mind. Many a time she'd say, "I've had it up to here with men.""

Being new in town made it difficult for us to make friends, even at school everyone was wary. Kids were warned off for hanging around with me. So for the first few months, I was pretty much on my own.

To pass the time and stay sane, I'd ride my bike out of town. I'd go into the bush and find interesting places to explore. I remember one particular Easter Monday like it was yesterday.

I'd decided to check out a place some of the local kids said was great for swimming. With a name like Hanging Tree Gorge, I figured the long ride out there would be worthwhile.

I found out it got that name when a black tracker called Darby was hanged from a large tree overlooking the Six Mile Creek. They reckon it had something to do with stolen dairy cows in the 1890s. Rough justice, eh? Accused of stealing cows and lynched without a trial.

Josh looks shocked. He puts his hands around his throat and says, "Hanged for pinching cows? Brian can't be hanged, can he?"

Young Josh's mind is running wild with horrible thoughts. I assure him: "Nah, they don't do that stuff anymore, thank God. Anyway, back to the story."
For that time of year, it was warmer than usual. Having to push my bike up a few hills meant I was sure hanging out for a swim.

A sign pointed the way down a narrow sandy track. It read:

'Hanging Tree Gorge – Swimming Prohibited – by order of the Historical Society'.

I was all sweaty, so I didn't pay any heed to the sign. I later learned neither did anyone else. Besides, who in hell were the Historical Society – telling folks they couldn't swim?

Anyway, the track gradually got narrower, overrun by thick bush. Then, as I rounded a right-hand bend, I saw a towering rocky outcrop overlooking the bush and the creek. It had a flat top with scrub on both sides. It wasn't too high and looked like it would make a great diving platform. At the bottom of the gorge ran the Six Mile Creek veering left around the outcrop.

I stopped, got off my bike and looked down the bank. It was pretty steep, and I skated to the bottom with my bike. The creek narrowed where a huge tree had fallen. I wondered if it might have been the hanging tree.

The widest section of the creek was up past the rocky platform. I dropped my bike and walked across the tree trunk straddling the creek. It was hilly on both sides and steeper on the side coming in. Through the bush, there were sandy tracks all over the place.

I went down to the edge of the creek. Putting a toe in the water, I discovered it was surprisingly warm and shallow. I decided to go up to the flat rocky area to see if it was much deeper and safe to jump off.

Puffing as I reached the top, I stopped to get my breath. Taking in the view, I saw that the creek snaked around thick bush and disappeared behind a row of tree-topped hills.

Looking down, I couldn't see the bottom and reckoned it was safe. So it was off with the shirt and shorts and on with the 'Speedos'.

I'd gone to the edge again to check the depth when suddenly a rock bounced out of the bush. I wheeled around and slipped over the edge. Hitting the water, I blacked out because the deeper water was so cold."
I deliberately stop my story here and cough to clear my dry throat, saying: "Hey, it's thirsty work telling stories, Josh. Do you want another drink?"

Josh rolls his eyes. "Aw! Come on, Pete, don't stop now. What happened next?"

At this point, I know I have him hooked. I like teasing the kids a bit, eh? Just like the TV soaps, where they leave you hanging on some important scene or painfully draw the story out. Anyway, I'm wandering. "Where was I?"

"Oh yes, next thing I know, I'm lying on the bank coughing up heaps of water and a blonde-haired, blue-eyed young guy is standing over me." He says, "Hey mate! Are you alright?"

I sit up and spit out more water. "I dunno. I think so. What happened?"

He points up at the outcrop and says, "I seen you slip off them rocks. Man! Was that a belly flop or what? It must've knocked the wind out of you."

He helps me to my feet, and I say, "I'm Peter Gannon. I could've drowned if you hadn't been here. I reckon you saved my life, eh?"

He shrugged. "It's nothin' really. I already know who you are. But guess what? If we lived in Saudi Arabia, I'd become part of your family – like brothers. Yeah, that's what we are now, we're brothers, right?"

I didn't know how to respond. "Right… umm, errr… but I don't know you."

The lad stuck up his hand and we gave each other a 'high-five'.

"Kurt Hoganhoffer. My Dad's family have been in this area for nearly one hundred years. We own the Rolling Hills Dairy. It's the big one along the highway, on the south side of town."

I was so happy. Not only had I beaten the Grim Reaper, but I'd also found a friend. I discovered later that Kurt's Dad owned just about everything in town and was unofficially the mayor. Whatever he said went.

Even though Kurt was eighteen months older than me, we met again the next day at school. He had another kid hanging around him all the time. This kid was short and dumpy looking with red hair. Never found out his last name, but everyone called him Scooter.

Something wasn't quite right with Scooter. I think he had Down's syndrome. There are two things I remember about Scooter. Firstly, he had those squinty eyes that sort of smiled at you when he laughed. Secondly, his nickname came from a scooter routine. He'd cock the wrist of his right hand twice, go VRROMM, VRROMM and say, 'See ya,' and then run off with an annoying screeching sound.

Kurt introduced us. "Scooter, this is Pete. He's one of us now. A brother, 'cos I saved his arse at the Gorge."

Scooter pulled a face, "But Colonel Hogan, he can't be a brother. He's not a 'Blood' – or done the secret."

I had bugger-all idea what he was going on about and must've had a strange look on my face.

Kurt set me straight: "It's alright Pete. To be a Blood Bro you have to go through a special ceremony and be given a ritual name from Hogan's Heroes. Mine's Colonel Hogan and we call the school Stalag 13."

It all sounded a bit weird. With some hesitation, I said, "Gee, I dunno. What sort of ceremony is it?"

Scooter pointed at me, saying, "It's a secret between Bloods. If you want to know then you have to become one. That's right Colonel Hogan. Ain't that right, eh, eh?"
Kurt smiled. "Yeah, Scooter's right. You have no choice. You have to become one of us, 'cos of what happened at the Gorge."

There I was, pulled in two directions. Kurt was pressuring me into something I wasn't sure about. But at the same time, I was desperate for friends. As I didn't have any, I couldn't afford to be fussy, eh?

At the time I thought it strange. Why was a smart guy like Kurt mucking around with such a sad case as Scooter? It didn't take long to find out the answer.

One of the teachers, Miss Marshall, happened to pass the drinking fountain. She stopped to have a drink. Kurt winked at me and whispered something to Scooter. He nodded and with his cheeky smile, he looked around before quietly approaching Miss Marshall from behind. Then he faked a fall to the ground, under her feet.

She jumped and spun around.

"My goodness, Gordon, are you alright?" she asked, helping him to his feet.

Scooter rushed back to Kurt all 'hyper' and panting like a dog. He kind'a danced around, flapping his hands.

"Colonel Hogan she... she's got pink undies.

"Kurt looked at me with a big cheesy grin and said, "I dunno, you're a bloody pervert, aren't ya Scooter?"

I thought to myself, does he think he's smart using poor Scooter like that, or is he grinning 'cos he's got one over the teacher?

The end-of-lunch siren went off with a wail. Kurt leaned his arm on my shoulder, saying, "Okay Pete, how's about we meet you Saturday morning in front of the Post Office? Then me and Scooter will take you to our secret spot to do the initiation."

Curious, I asked, "Okay, but, where's this secret spot?"

Scooter flapped his hands in front of my face and chanted, "We're not allowed to t-e-l-l."

Kurt lifted his arm from my shoulder. "Yeah, Scooter's right. Just be there and don't be late."

Scooter hopped on his bike, cocked his wrist twice: "VRROMM, VRROMM – See ya – Scr-e-e-c-h," and ran off to class.

That Friday night, I was so excited to be joining a gang, I had trouble sleeping.

Keen to get started, I was up early the next morning organising some munchies for the trip. I had no idea where we were going or how long it would take.

I rode into town and got to the Post Office earlier than agreed. To fill in time I did circles on my bike out the front, daydreaming about satanic initiations and wondering what secret cults do to blokes being initiated.

A shout broke my daydreaming. It was Scooter, on his bike.

"Yoo-Hoo, Pete," he called, taking a deep breath. "Kurt says he can't meet us here. He has to get some medicine for his Mum. But we're allowed to go around later."

After a sleepless night and looking forward to the adventure, I felt annoyed and snapped back, "Well, what do we do now?"

Scooter smiled with his squinty eyes and gushed, "Come back to my place. I got a big stack of Nudie books. D'ya wanna see 'em?"

I was stunned. But then again, nothing was normal with Scooter.

"Where do you live?" I asked.

"Come on, Pete, follow me." Scooter cocked his wrist twice: "VRROMM, VRROMM, Scr-e-e-c-h."

Focused on my memory of that morning, I almost didn't hear Kate's question.

"Excuse me, Pete, why do you say Scooter wasn't normal? My son has a girl called Marie in his class with Down's syndrome and she's a very happy girl. She does all the things the other kids do at school."

I have to think for a minute, gathering my thoughts.

"Well, in those times, Kate, kids like Scooter were thought of as backward and called 'Mongoloid'. We didn't know any better. It was only in the 1960s they discovered it was a genetic disorder."

"Maybe. But it's disgusting to call someone that label when they can't help it."

"Yes, I get your point Kate and thankfully times have changed."

Meanwhile, Josh is getting fidgety and says, "Can we get back to your story as I want to know all about the ritual stuff."

"Okay, Josh."

"We left the main street and headed for the edge of town. We crossed the railway and rode over the wooden Six Mile Bridge. Then, veered right onto a well-worn path which ran along the bank of the creek.

A large sign pointed the way to the entrance of the Pomona Caravan Park. We stopped outside an old caravan with a canvas annex attached.

Sitting under a big shady tree was an old lady reading a book. We dropped our bikes on the lawn in front of the caravan.

Glancing up, the old lady said, "Who's your friend?"

Scooter stopped in his tracks and replied, "He's new from school, Gran. We're goin' over to Kurt's after we get a drink."

The old lady put the book down in her lap and in a tired voice said, "I don't know why you hang around Kurt Hoganhoffer – that kid's no good, I tell you."

She picked up the book again and muttered, "But nobody listens to me."

We stepped up into the caravan and Scooter stooped down, opening a small fridge. He turned his head, saying, "We only got water and cordial, 'cos Gran says cool drinks are bad for you and cost too much."

Scooter poured the drinks, making a mess in the process.

Taking a sip, it was sickly sweet – way too much cordial. While Scooter cleaned up his mess, I was thinking, maybe this is not his home and he's just visiting. Curious, I asked, "So where do you live?"

Turning around, he looked out the door and pointed to the annex. "That's my room," he proudly announced. "Gran says I'm lucky, 'cos not many kids have a room under the stars."

We went into the annex. All Scooter had was a bed and an old, battered wardrobe. Scooter looked out the doorway and closed the flap.
He giggled. "Do you want to see my Nudie books?"

I replied, "Whatever." I was still in shock, thinking this poor kid's got bugger-all, yet he's always happy.

Scooter reached up to the top of the wardrobe and pulled down a stack of Playboy and Hustler magazines wrapped in a crumpled, brown paper carry bag.

Lifting the magazines out, he said, "These used to belong to Grandpa before he left."

I asked, "Where did he go?"

Scooter blinked in a bemused fashion. "Oh, Pete, he died. But he gave these to me before he died. He said at his age, it was the only pleasure he had left and maybe I could get some pleasure from them too."

I was thinking, what a weird inheritance, eh? The old guy must've felt sorry for Scooter, being, you know, short-changed with all his problems.

Scooter gave me a couple of his mags to look at. But tell you the truth, I felt uncomfortable and flicked through them fast without paying much attention. 'Cos I was thinking to myself, how come he's living in this caravan with his Gran? What about his Mum and Dad? What happened to them?

I put the mags down without comment. Scooter grabbed them as if they were priceless and put them back, saying, "Let's go. We can't keep the Colonel waiting."

We left Scooter's canvas bedroom and picked up our bikes. "Gran, we're going now," he called out. Then, cocking his wrist twice, he shouted his usual VRROMM, VRROMM, Scr-e-e-c-h, as we set off to Kurt's place.

I noticed his Gran did not look up from her book as we rode back across the railway line.

Scooter's situation had me curious. It took me a while before I summoned up the courage to ask, "Scooter, how come you live with your Gran?"

"Mum was very sick when I was born."

"Where's your Mum now?"

"She's in a special hospital. Gran won't let me visit, since the last time. It's the drugs."

I decided not to ask about his Dad or anything else. Each answer seemed to make his life more bizarre.

We pedalled out of town in silence until Scooter shouted, "There's Kurt's place. You can't miss it."

I looked across to where Scooter was pointing; two tall, white pillars guarded the dairy entrance. A fabulous two-storey mansion stood at the end of the drive. Wow, that's pretty impressive, I thought, comparing it to our old rental and Scooter's canvas annex.

Kurt was walking down the side of the house as we pedalled up their driveway. His bike was lying next to the marbled front steps.

It was a lot to take in. Around the property, lush-green pastures stood out. Giant sprinklers with rubber tyres were going, swish, swish, swish in looping arcs. Large sheds dotted the landscape, along with various bits of machinery – all weird shapes and sizes.

My immediate thoughts were: boy! Kurt's lucky. His folks are absolutely loaded.

When we approached the house, there was a movement on the upstairs balcony. A woman appeared in a dressing gown. She lurched forward to the railing with a glass in one hand and leaned over. Her long blonde hair looked untidy, and her cleavage was showing. She took a swig from the glass.

Scooter looked at me and nodded knowingly. "That's Kurt's Mum and that's her medicine." As Kurt reached us, she called out, "Kurt!" He took no notice.

"Kurt, my baby! Why are you going off with that half-wit and leaving me here all on my own?"
Kurt put his hand on Scooter's shoulder and said, "Don't let her bother you. She doesn't know what she's saying when she's like that."

She shouted again. "Kurt! Are you listening to me?"

As Kurt picked up his bike, I heard him hiss through clenched teeth, "I hate you."

He wheeled his bike a few paces to bring the pedal to the top and waved to us. "Let's get out of here guys."

Scooter jumped on his bike and cocked his wrist twice: "VRROOMM, VRROOMM, Scr-e-e-c-h."

We were away again. We followed Kurt as he pedalled quickly down the drive with his Mum calling, "Kurt, come back! Don't go. Mummy needs you."

By the time we reached the front gates, my mind had done a complete 180. A short time ago I'd been envious of Kurt. Now I felt sorry for him. As we turned left, I asked, "Where are we going?"

Riding ahead of us Kurt looked back at me and grinned, "Patience Bro. You'll see soon."

Chapter 2
Blood Ritual

After a couple of kilometres, the flat paddocks became hilly, and the road carved its way through them. We were coasting downhill around a bend when Scooter yelled, "There's the track."

On our right, I saw a dusty track veering off the main road. It seemed to disappear into a tree-lined tunnel. After we passed under the trees, we had to stand in our saddles and pump the pedals hard to follow the track up a large hill. We stopped at the crest to catch our breath.

Getting off his bike, Kurt pushed it to the top of the rise. Puffing, Scooter and I followed.

We reached the top of the hill just as a large black cloud slid in front of the sun. At the same time, a cold breeze sprang up.

Through the gloom, I could make out a rocky outcrop. It looked surreal; a flat section in the middle guarded by huge boulders. It reminded me of a magazine picture, Stonehenge. Looking at the brooding landscape, I felt a chill run up my spine.

I muttered to myself, "So this is the secret spot."

The atmosphere made me think of Picnic at Hanging Rock, an eerie movie I'd seen. Horrible thoughts raced through my mind. What if these two had lured me here to do something else? Maybe they were Satanic and planned to sacrifice me.

A strong gust of wind howled through the rocky outcrop, tearing at my hair. I was thinking that perhaps we should forget the whole thing, until Kurt pointed to the view.

"Now you know why we chose this place. You can see for ages, even out past the Headland."

The views were impressive enough for me to forget my earlier panic. Then, as if to reassure me, the sun came out of hiding and in an instant, the dark inky ocean water turned bright turquoise blue.

We dropped our bikes and took turns swigging from my water bottle. No one said much. We were getting our breath back and psyching ourselves up for the ceremony. Kurt was the first to move. He walked over to the flat rock in the middle of 'Stonehenge'. He took out a pocketknife and, surprisingly, a small Bible. Kneeling, he placed the Bible on the ground with the pocketknife on top of it and gestured for Scooter and me to come closer.

Dramatically, Kurt held out his arms and chanted, "By the powers invested in me and as God is my witness, I now commence the Blood Brothers' ritual."

Kurt picked up the knife and cut into the palm of his hand. He allowed blood to spill onto the rocky ground and chanted, "With my blood, I anoint the Earth and my Blood Brothers, so that we become one."

He motioned to Scooter to hold out his hand. He flinched as Kurt jabbed it into his palm. Kurt joined palms with Scooter for a moment to let their blood mix. Then I held out my hand, determined not to flinch. Kurt looked at me squarely in the eyes. He cut deeply into my hand and smirked. He was enjoying the drama of it all – like a cult leader presiding over his flock.

He grabbed our hands and joined our three palms together chanting, "With the mixing of our blood we are now brothers and true to each other – forever."

He paused and then said, "Now Pete, you must recite the oath and be named. Repeat after me, I, Peter Gannon, after revealing my secret will become a Blood Brother and will keep the bond strong and true, no matter what."

After reciting the oath, I asked," What's the secret for, Kurt?"
Kurt grinned. "The secret is to make sure none of us snitches on each other. It's got to be something you don't want anybody to know about."

I was caught on the hop. I couldn't think of any secrets that would impress Kurt. The only thing that came to mind was pinching some lollies from a Deli. On the way home I'd felt guilty and chucked them away.

Stalling for time, I said: "Have to think about it, Kurt. Maybe you or Scooter go first; you guys already know yours."

Scooter seemed delighted. "Oh, oh, me first," he said, flapping his arms around and making panting sounds.

Stopping my story there, I arose from my 'old faithful' planter's chair and announced, "Guess what Josh? I'm going to do what the TV soaps do. I'm not going to reveal the secrets just yet – got to keep you interested."

"That's not fair," he protested. "Why can't you tell us now?"

"Patience, dear Cuz. All will be revealed in good time. Besides, secrets are for keeping, don't you think?"

Josh pulled a sour face. "I suppose so. But you have to promise you will tell us."

I put up my hand as if under oath, "I promise."

Josh crossed his arms and chanted, "Cross your heart and hope to die."

After playfully holding him in suspense, I say, "Okay, okay, already. I get the message."

I took my empty can into the kitchen, returned to 'old faithful' and gathered my thoughts, continuing from after we'd agreed to share our deepest darkest secrets.

Kurt was presiding and announced the other 'formalities'.

"Okay," he said. "There are two more formalities left. Since your secret relates to poetry and the French are poets, we will call you Le Beau after the Frenchman in Hogan's Heroes."

Kurt dived into a bag tied to his handlebars and pulled out a bottle of whiskey. "Hey Bro's," he said, waving the bottle in front of us, "This is from Dad's drinks cabinet. We all have to skull."

He handed it to Scooter first, who in the excitement of the occasion, took a quick swig of whiskey and spilt it down the front of his shirt.

Kurt snatched the bottle back, almost yelling at Scooter, "Hey! Don't waste it. That stuff's expensive."

Scooter wiped his mouth with his sleeve and giggled.

Kurt handed me the bottle. I decided to take a big swig to impress them. It burned all the way down and took my breath away. I promptly threw up, much to Kurt's delight, while Scooter clapped his hands and danced on the spot.

From that ritual day, we began hanging out together after school and mucking around on weekends.

We spent a lot of time swimming at Hanging Tree Gorge. Kurt was always in charge, telling us what to do. But at the time I didn't mind too much. It was better than being on your own, eh?

Josh had a question: "Hey Pete, what's Hogan's Heroes?" he asked, reminding me of the generation gap between us and may have not seen the iconic TV show.

"Oh yeah, I said. "It was a TV Sit-com about Allied prisoners in a German prisoner of war camp called Stalag 13.

"It was propaganda because the Americans always won and made the Germans look stupid. Colonel Hogan was the American in charge and Sergeant Schulz was a dumb, clumsy guard who used to say 'I see *nothzing*, I hear *nothzing*, I say *nothzing*'.

"Now you know why Kurt gave Scooter that name. Anyway, let me get back to the story."

One day after we'd been swimming, Kurt decided we should warm up by lying on the rocky platform above the swimming hole. He wanted to spy on anyone who might be around.
We'd been sunning ourselves for a while and had dozed off when we heard a splash. We rolled over, crawled lizard-like to the edge of the rocky platform. Peering over it, we saw a dark-skinned bloke swimming naked along the gorge.

"That's Donny Buckle, the deaf-mute Abo," Kurt whispered. "Let's steal his gear and see what happens."

Kurt barked out his orders to Scooter. "Schulz, sneak down and grab his gear. But make sure he doesn't see you."

Scooter giggled excitedly and shouted out, "Ja Vol, Mein Herr. I know nothzin…"

"Shoosh Scooter," Kurt scolded.

Scooter lifted his second finger to his lips and feigned 'ssshh'. He rolled away from the edge of the rocky platform and crouching low disappeared into the bush. We peered over the edge again. Donny was swimming towards us. We ducked our heads until we heard his splashing fading away from us. Lifting our heads, we could see Scooter creeping across the fallen tree to where Donny's clothes were neatly draped over a bush.

Curious, I whispered to Kurt, "Who's this Donny guy?"

Kurt whispered back, "The loser's a deaf-mute from birth. His folks didn't want him, so Pastor Carey from the Holy Spirit Mission took him in.

"My Dad says the Pastor's always suckin' up his arse for donations. The only donation I'd like to make is to that spunky Rachel, the Pastor's daughter. She's the biggest tease in town, but her Daddy don't know."

Kurt tapped my arm and pointed to where Scooter had reached Donny's clothes. As Scooter grabbed Donny's blue shirt, Kurt chuckled, "Let's make things interesting."

He picked up a rock and with a grunt hurled it in Donny's direction.

The rock splashed down in front of him. Donny stopped suddenly. Treading water, he glanced around anxiously. Seeing Scooter, he started thrashing madly towards him, making weird grunting sounds. Kurt laughed. "Look out, Scooter," he yelled. "Let's get out of here."

With Donny's shirt in his hand, Scooter scrambled back across the fallen tree.

Kurt and I scattered: we didn't wait to see what Donny might do. I grabbed my bike and charged up the sandy track. At the top, I jumped on it and pedalled furiously away, not bothering about the others.

It wasn't until school morning break the next day that I caught up with them. Both were behaving strangely. They didn't even ask where I'd gone.

Scooter was unusually quiet – not his bubbly self – and kept looking at the ground.

Kurt bailed me up against the toilet block wall and forcefully said, "Remember, we're Blood Brothers. Anything we do is kept within the circle."

I looked at Kurt and replied, "You know that, so where's the problem?"

Kurt grabbed my shirt, saying: "If anyone asks, we were never at the Gorge. Got it?"

Just then, the siren sounded so we moved back to our classes.

I was left wondering what happened after I took off. It had to be something to do with Scooter.

Maybe the deaf-mute caught Scooter and dobbed him in; yeah, that must've been it, I thought.

At lunchtime, a rumour spread around the school, like wildfire, that something happened at the swimming hole and Donny had been arrested. What for, nobody seemed to know.

After school, I waited as usual for Kurt and Scooter, but they didn't show. I decided to head for Tony's Milk Bar. I had some change I'd been saving from my lunch money and was hanging out for icecream.

While standing around the side of the Milk Bar giving a Drumstick ice cream cone a good tongue lashing, I heard two ladies from the church, standing out the front of the Milk Bar discussing an attack at the swimming hole.

You could rely on Maggie Smith and old Mrs Jones to know what was going on around town.

I stood very still behind the lattice partition and eavesdropped.

I heard Mrs Jones say, "I told you! Rachel Carey's a floozy. I knew something like this attack would happen to her."

"You're right, Mrs Jones. I don't feel sorry for her. It's Pastor Carey I feel for; such a fine, God-fearing man. What did he do to deserve this?"

"That daughter of his flaunts herself all the time in short skirts and tight blouses," Mrs Jones said. "It was bound to come to no good.

"And the deaf-mute: I knew he had the devil in him. That's the thanks the Pastor gets for taking him in.

"Just because the swimming hole is a long way out of town, people think they can go skinny dippin' there. But I've heard it's a place frequented by perverts.

"I don't know what the girl was thinking – swimming with no clothes on and in broad daylight. That's asking for trouble."

"You're right," Maggie agreed. "I heard that Sergeant Mike Collis got the call about the assault and on his way out to investigate, found Donny wandering along the main road back into town. Would you believe it? Donny was partly naked too. Stripped to the waist, with no shirt!"

Mrs Jones had more to say: "Maggie, who knows what went on? I tell you, all these strangers coming into our town means trouble."

I finished my Drumstick and as I put the wrapper in the bin, the two women realised I could have heard them. They quickly moved away.

I jumped back on my bike and headed home thinking about what I'd overheard.

It seemed like a lot happened after I left the swimming hole. I felt uneasy. Something didn't add up.
If Donny attacked Rachel, why were Kurt and Scooter behaving so strangely? Then I thought, well maybe they knew about it but didn't want it known they were out there.

I knew why Donny didn't have his shirt on, 'cos Scooter stole it.

Was Kurt protecting Scooter from any hassles?

The next day at school, I caught up with Kurt, to find out what happened.

"I know why you were so touchy yesterday," I said. "I found out Donny 'did it' with that Rachel bird after we took his stuff: seems she went Nicky swimming after we left."

Kurt grabbed me roughly by the shirt. This was becoming an annoying habit.

"Don't you get it?" he hissed. "We were never there! Got it?"

I took hold of his arms. "Let go! I don't understand. Surely it can't matter whether we were there or not? Donny's been arrested!"

Kurt let go and smoothed out my shirt. "Sorry mate. I'm just looking out for Scooter, that's all.

"He flips out every time he sees a cop. Did you know his Mum's a druggie and they came and took her away? Besides, you know Scooter's a pervert and tells everyone he's got nudie books. Now how would that look to the cops?"

We parted company.

What Kurt said made sense, I thought. It tied in with what Scooter had told me.

Everything settled down between us, but we never went back to the swimming hole.

It soon became obvious that things between Kurt and Scooter weren't the same either, even though Kurt kept saying he was "looking out for him".

The uneasiness between Kurt and me boiled over after a special court hearing came up. Can't think what it's called. But it was to decide whether Donny's case should go ahead.

On the day after the hearing, I decided to catch up with Kurt at lunchtime because I remembered that his Dad was going to the court.

"Hi Kurt, how ya going?" I asked.

"I suppose you want to know what happened with the court."

"Yeah, just curious."

"Well, the Magistrate decided Donny has to face trial.

"The police sergeant found Donny walking along the road without his blue shirt on and had evidence the shirt was used in the attack. *But you can't say nothin'! And you know why.*"

"Yeah, I know, I know – the pact. See you later."

I left with a lot of unanswered questions.

Scooter had Donny's blue shirt. Did he dump it when we bolted? Did Donny get his shirt back and hang around, after?

Kurt and Scooter were acting weird. Could they have been with the girl? Their behaviour sure didn't make any sense to me.

On my way home that Friday afternoon, I spotted Scooter's bike lying on the grass verge near the oval. It was strange, 'cos he loved that bike and always had it chained up.

I stopped, got off my bike and wheeled it across the oval to the Change Rooms. I heard someone sobbing from behind them. When I looked around the corner, I saw Scooter sitting on the ground, hugging his knees, rocking back and forth, tears streaming down his face.

I asked, "Hey Scooter! What's wrong matey?"

"I'm not your mate anymore," he sobbed.

"Kurt said he saw me with Donny's shirt. He's kicked me out of Hogan's Heroes. He reckons I'm a sex pervert. He said I make him feel sick. He says he'll tell the police my secret."

I didn't know what to say, but I wanted to hear his side of the story.

"Scooter, what did you do?"

Scooter jumped to his feet and ran at me shouting, "You're like him! I hate you!"

He pushed me hard in the chest and I fell backwards. Before I could get up and say anything more, he ran to his bike and rode off.

I wanted to follow him, but I had to head home and help Mum pack. We were going away that weekend to visit relatives in Brisbane.

During our visit to Brisbane, I stood on broken glass and Mum thought I should have my foot checked out before school on Monday. So I turned up at school halfway through assembly just as the Headmaster was saying grief counselling was available for any students affected.

Affected? By what, I wondered.

While the assembly was breaking up, Kurt came over to me. He looked serious.

"I guess you heard the terrible news," he said. "You know I found him."

I shrugged: "Nope. Don't know what you're talking about."

Kurt shook his head: "Scooter."

I felt as if I'd been kicked in the stomach.

"Kurt! Are you saying Scooter's dead? Oh my God! How?"

Kurt grabbed my arm and led me to a quiet spot. "Scooter hanged himself at the Gorge," he whispered.

I shook my head, grasped my throat; all I could get out was: "S-h-i-t!" Kurt looked around to check we could not be overheard.

Still whispering, he said: "Don't say nothin', but Scooter left a note. He said he was sorry for what he done."

I blinked and shook my head again. "No! He can't have done that?"

Kurt picked up a rock and angrily hurled it onto the oval.

"Yes, he could. But I blame that bitch Rachel: parading around in shorts; swimming nude.

"You know he got all excited by 'hoochie-coochie' stuff. You know about his secret and all those nudie books he had. It's her fault he's done himself in."

"Shit, what about Donny? We have to give the cops his note."

Kurt shrugged. "I can't. I got rid of it. I reckon Scooter's had enough trouble."

Looking him in the eyes, I said, "But Kurt, that's not right."

He just shrugged again. "Right or wrong, that's the way it is. Best leave it to the courts."

Kurt was being matter of fact. I wondered how he could be so cool about it all while I was 'packing-it'.

My heart was pounding. "But what if they say Donny's guilty?"

"Just remember, we're Blood Brothers, our blood mixed. You can't go against that. If you do, I'll tell the Headmaster your secret."

The thought occurred to me that getting pinged for my secret was nothing compared to what had happened to Scooter; or what might happen to Donny.

By this time, I was angry and blasted him. "I don't care what you do, Kurt. It ain't right!"

Kurt glared at me with cruel eyes. "Listen Pete, you wouldn't be here without me. Remember, I saved your arse; you would've drowned. You owe me. Nothing's going to bring Scooter back. But if you want to make something of it, then I can dob you into the cops, too. Guess who they'd believe?"

I knew the answer. His Dad would make sure it was me who'd lose out.

I tried to push past Kurt and leave. But he blocked my path.

"Piss off," I hissed.

He stood aside but as I left, he was shouting at me. The last thing I heard was: "Remember what I said. Think real hard before you do something you'll regret."

Kurt was no mate, I realised. My guts were churning in reaction to his threat.

Back in the classroom, I couldn't shake a sense of being 'boxed in' by the situation. I had to get out of there, so I told the teacher I was coming down with something and needed to go home.

She asked, "Is your Mum home?"

"No," I said. "She's at work."

The teacher replied, "I'm not having one of my students go home to an empty house. I want you to go to the sickbay and see how you feel in an hour. If you don't feel any better, I'll phone your Mum to come and get you."

I didn't go to the sick room. All I wanted to do was go home and I didn't care if the teachers found out, so I took off.

Looking quite stunned, as he hears this part of my story, Josh pipes up:

"Wow Pete, I can't believe Scooter did that. I was getting to like him. I guess you never know, eh? Maybe that's why he hanged himself. But you haven't said what happened with that chick, Rachel?"

Kate sighs, "After all this time, there are people who still say she caused the attack. They're a bunch of bloody narrow-minded bigots."

I tell Josh he's right to ask about Rachel. Here's how the town responded to her misfortune.

Pomona was abuzz with opinions about her. Fingers pointed at her clothing style and people questioned why she'd gone swimming alone, in the nude.

Rachel was pretty. She had blonde hair, blue eyes and was an early bloomer. She was only sixteen but looked about eighteen and wore sexy gear whenever she could get away with it. She was a free spirit – a bit too lively for her Dad, Pastor Carey.

From what I was able to piece together, she was causing him a lot of stress.

I overheard him talking with Maggie Smith one day. "I can't help feeling that Rachel brought this on herself with her wayward ways," he said. "It's the devil's work, alright.

"I believe God rewards those doing His good works, and God knows I've given so much to this Parish. Has my work been undone because of one parishioner's shameful moment of weakness? Donny, I mean. Yet at the same time, I fear I've blamed the whole mess on Rachel.

"God willing, time will heal our wounds."

Recalling the effect of the attack on Pastor Carey, I pause for a moment to catch my breath. But impatient Josh has my school-wagging exploit on his mind.

"What happened when you wagged school? Did you get found out?"

"No Josh. Mum covered for me." Let me continue.

I felt out of it when I got home. I was so tired I flopped into a big chair and almost dozed off. Then a whole bunch of questions began racing through my mind.

Why was Scooter crying behind the change rooms?

What happened over the weekend, while I was away?

Did Kurt do something to Scooter to make him feel so bad?

I still wasn't sure who attacked Rachel. Was it Donny? Was it Scooter? And if it wasn't Scooter, why would he kill himself?

What if Kurt was lying about the note?

None of it made sense. I couldn't come up with any answers.

Feeling exhausted I drifted into a strange space, neither awake nor asleep.

Suddenly I found myself lifting off the chair. There was the sound of the wind rushing past me and through my hair. Next thing I knew I was flying over the spot where we'd held the Blood Brothers ritual. It wasn't scary or anything. I could see the coastline and the breakers across the coastal bushland against the deep blue sky. The colours were incredibly vivid.

Then, like an eagle, I was flying above the Hanging Tree Gorge and down the Six Mile creek. On the rocky diving platform, someone was waving. When I got closer, I could see it was Scooter smiling and waving with both hands, in his funny way. A feeling of peace and calm came over me.

As I came back to reality, I thought maybe Scooter had found peace. But I was annoyed: there he was showing me that he was alright. Well, what about the bloody mess he'd left behind? And me, stuck right in the middle of it.

Scooter's funeral was held the following week, and Mum gave me permission to wag school so I could attend. Because I hadn't been to a funeral before, she took time off work to come with me.

Despite what Scooter did, I felt sorry for him.

We didn't go to the Funeral Home, just to the Crematorium chapel. There was only a small group of people paying their final respects.

In one group, I recognised Scooter's Grandma. She was with some people I didn't know. I assumed they were relatives. Although I tried to catch her eye, she paid no attention to me.

Pastor Carey was there with his family, but I didn't see Rachel. The Headmaster and the Deputy Headmistress also attended.

Just before the hearse arrived, I noticed Kurt lurking around in the background. So did Scooter's Grandma. She whispered something to a man in a black suit who immediately walked up to Kurt, grasped his shoulder, and ushered him towards the front gate.

I couldn't hear what the man said, but when Kurt looked back, there was fear on his face. Kurt ran through the cemetery gate and disappeared behind a brick wall. He'd been thrown out of Scooter's funeral.

I wondered, what does that old lady know about Kurt that I don't?

Inside the chapel, Pastor Carey got up to speak about Scooter. He said, "God chose a difficult assignment for Scooter in this life, yet despite the many problems he had to deal with, he was always a cheerful and happy person."

That was so true. Pastor Carey didn't mention how Scooter died. Instead, he simply said his life had been cut short and wished him well on his journey to a better place.

It took me several months to come to terms with what happened to Scooter, and Kurt's behaviour.

I avoided Kurt like the plague. He was avoiding me, too.

I never went back to Hanging Tree Gorge again. I couldn't. The mental image of Scooter swinging there gave me the creeps.

All these years later, sitting in my front room with Kate and Josh, I feel the same cold tingle down my spine. I pause, shaking my shoulders in a shudder at the thought of it.

Josh hasn't noticed my discomfort and wants to push on with 'what happened next'.

"Pete, what about that Donny bloke," he asks. "What did you do about him?"

"I didn't do anything. I was afraid of what Kurt might do. Besides, Kurt kept reminding me that he saved my life. I sort of respected him for being a friend to Scooter and, after all, we were Blood Brothers. I thought that if I left things as they were, it would all go away.

"That's pretty much how things went, even at the Coroner's Inquest into Scooter's death. I found out the Coroner's finding was death by misadventure – whatever that meant. I worried about Donny: if he was innocent, he might get off and that would be the end of my hassles, eh Josh?"

Chapter 3
The Courts

It's funny how some things in life that you try to forget keep coming back.

Our major school assignment the following year turned out to be Democracy in Action.

As Donny's trial was coming up, I decided to do mine on the courts. You know, stuff about juries and all that.

To do it properly I'd need to attend a hearing and see exactly what went on. Plus I'd find out if he was guilty or not. That way I'd get a day off school too. It didn't seem like schoolwork at the time.

On the day of Donny's hearing, I rode my bike down to the Bruce highway and hid it in the bush behind the bus stop. Then I sat on the road verge waiting for the bus to come. My mind was miles away when a faded, green four-wheel-drive Land Rover pulled up next to me.

The driver wound down the window and shouted, "Hey son, do you want a lift?"

Standing up, I shook my head – no. "Mum says I have to catch the bus."

The man understood why I was reluctant and replied, "I'm Bill Bladelock. I work for Mr Hoganhoffer at Rolling Hills Dairy. I've seen you knocking around with young Kurt. I'm going all the way to Noosa: your choice son."

What he said made me feel comfortable, so I opened the door and climbed aboard. "Thanks Mister, I'm going to Noosa too." He asked, "What's yer name, son?"

"Peter Gannon, but you can call me Pete."

He glanced over at me, "Well Pete, it's yer lucky day, then. How come yer not goin' to school?"

"I've got permission to sit in on a court trial at the District Court. It's for a study I'm doing on Democracy."

He nodded. "School of life, eh? What's the case about?"

"There's this deaf-mute Aboriginal bloke called Donny Buckle; he's been charged with attacking a girl at Hanging Tree Gorge."

Bill nodded again. "Yeah, I heard about that; Pastor Carey's daughter. What's her name? Oh yes, Rachel. I reckon he did it. The way I heard it, the cops caught him straight afterwards. See here's the thing: you can't trust the *Darkies*."

Not knowing what to say, I just nodded back. I got a funny feeling this day was not going to be a good one: not for Donny and not for me.

It was becoming clear that Donny had the cards firmly stacked against him. His disability and the prejudice he faced would be obstacles in his fight for justice.

Neither of us spoke for a while. Then Bill said, "By the way, I haven't seen yer with Kurt lately? Yeah, and haven't seen that funny looking kid that used to hang around with Kurt, either."

I swallowed hard: "That... that funny-looking kid was Scooter. He died a while ago. He... he hanged himself at the swimming hole."

"Jesus," Bill exclaimed. "What is this place coming to? Used to be a quiet, safe place once. I blame it on all the 'weirdos' coming into town. What do you reckon?"

I shrugged, relieved to see a sign, Noosa 5km. Not long now, I thought. None too soon, as Bill was making me edgy.

He dropped me off outside the Courthouse and thanked me for

making a lonely trip enjoyable. Well, enjoyable for him, I thought.

Taking a deep breath, I marched up to a policeman standing out the front of the Courthouse.

"Hi there," I said in a dry, weak voice.

He looked down at me and replied, "Hello, young fellow. How can I help you?"

"I've… I've come from Pomona to watch a court case. But I don't know where to go."

The policeman straightened up and pointed, "Excellent, come to see Justice working. Just go through there, continue down the corridor until you see the double doors. There's a sign next to the door indicating the case to be heard. Go in and sit at the back to your right."

I nervously made my way down the corridor. When I got level with the doors, my stomach tightened. My earlier excitement and anticipation of the adventure suddenly vanished when I read the sign: Crown v Buckle.

I hesitated before pushing on the double doors. I thought, jeez, I don't think I want to go in now. I didn't have a choice, though. It was a school assignment – and I hoped I might find out whether Donny was guilty.

Peering inside, I could smell a stale, musty aroma from the wood panelling and the polished leather seats. The courtroom felt over-powering despite being empty and silent. I sat down and took in all its details.

Suddenly, the double doors flew open. Startled, I looked around. Two men wearing black silk gowns and white wigs entered. They were carrying big files and were too busy chatting to notice me.

They shuffled slowly down to the front, one of them remarking, "This case will be an absolute shoo-in. Legal Aid appointed old Humphrey to run the defendant's case."

The other Silk responded, "The old drunkard has trouble with normal clients. How's he going to handle the deaf-mute?"

"Well, it looks like three strikes and he's in. A drunk for a Barrister, a deaf-mute defendant and all we need is an all-white jury. We can't lose."

Moments later, one of the double doors slowly opened. A huge man with a red nose and a big belly limped in. He too was wearing a black silk gown and wig. I assumed he was Humphrey, Donny's Counsel.

While Humphrey was getting comfortable in his seat, a man in uniform led in a group of people. I found out later he was the Bailiff and the people he was leading in were candidates for the jury.

One by one, the candidates had their names and occupations called out. Stepping forward, they each placed their right hand on a Bible held by the Bailiff and recited the oath: "I will conscientiously try the issues on which my decision is required and decide them according to the evidence. I will also not disclose anything about the jury's deliberations other than as allowed or required by law. So help me God."

I was thinking, God help Donny.

Next, jury selection began.

A dark-skinned man stepped forward; the Prosecutor shouted, "Stand by," and the Bailiff pointed for him to stand away from the others. Jeez, I thought, Donny can't even have a member of his own race in the jury.

Humphrey was looking down at some papers; he lifted his head and glared at the Prosecutor.

The next person to walk forward was a woman; a schoolteacher.

I'm sure out for revenge, Humphrey shouted, "Challenge," and the schoolteacher was told to stand away from the others.

There were no more challenges after that.

Once the jury had taken the oath, they filed along rows of seats on the right-hand side of the courtroom and sat down. I counted twelve heads, all of them men.

The imposing but empty Judge's bench was on the opposite end.

Two Prosecutors sat on the left-hand side of a long table in front of the public gallery, with Humphrey on their right. Another door opened and Donny was led in by a man in uniform.

My heart jumped.

He was ushered into a box with a glass screen behind it, separating him from the public gallery. When Donny sat down, the man in uniform took a seat next to the box.

Three more people entered through the double doors and moved down to a bench in front of the Judge's box.

There was a low whisper in the court until the Court Clerk stood up. "Silence," he shouted. "All stand please, for Honourable Justice Sir William Hicks."

An imposing figure entered from a door behind the Judge's box. He bowed and everyone bowed back. When the Judge was seated, the Clerk gestured for everyone to sit.

He then announced: "Court is now in session for the hearing of the Crown versus Buckle.

The Prosecutor was quick to rise to his feet. "If your Honour pleases, my name is Chaney and I appear with my learned friend, Jones for the Crown."

Humphrey struggled to his feet and with one hand holding onto the bench mumbled, "If your Honour pleases, my name is Turner and I appear for the Respondent."

Josh interrupts me to ask, "Hey Big Cuz, how come you know all this? It sounds really scary, being in a court. How'd you remember all that stuff, and who's the Respondent?"

"I wouldn't have, Josh, except I took a tape deck in and recorded it. Wouldn't get away with that today with all the security, eh? I replayed it so many times it's indelibly imprinted on my brain. I managed to get a transcript of the case too and went over it a few times.

"In answer to your question, the Respondent is a legal word for the accused person being tried. Right, Kate?"

She nods approvingly.

Josh has another question. "How come that Chaney guy works for the 'Crown'. Shouldn't he be working for the 'People'?"

"Excellent question. Kate, you can answer this, since you're the *Legal-Eagle*."

"Okay," says Kate. "Australia is still under the English system of justice and part of the Commonwealth of Nations, ruled by a Monarch. It's different in the United States, which is a Republic with its own Constitution and President."

"That's great Kate. Now, let's get back to the courtroom. Where was I?"

Oh yes, the Crown Prosecutor stood up again and said, "If it may please your Honour, I shall outline the Crown's case against the accused. It shall be the Crown's contention that on April 16, 1978, the accused, after going swimming in the Six Mile Creek at Hanging Tree Gorge, later hid, and from that vantage point spied on Rachel Jane Carey as she removed her clothing and swam in the creek. I further submit that the accused stalked Miss Carey and placed his shirt over her head before assaulting her. The evidence, your Honour, is damning."

Suddenly, Donny jumped to his feet and pointed with both index fingers at his eyes. He then pointed his fingers towards the Judge and opened and closed them as if they were lips.

The Judge told Donny to sit down. Donny didn't budge. Instead, he pointed to his ears and turned both thumbs downwards.

Old Humphrey stood up and told the Court, "Your Honour, my client is a deaf-mute and because he's behind the bench cannot understand the proceedings."

"Mr Turner," the Judge exclaimed, "Why hasn't your client got an interpreter? How in the devil can justice be served when your client doesn't even know what's going on? And what's more, has to take it upon himself to point this out to the court."

Humphrey shifted his stance uncomfortably and replied, "Your Honour, I was unable to secure the services of an interpreter in time for this hearing. However, my client is well versed in lip-reading. May it please your Honour, can the accused be moved so that he can read the lips of the Learned Counsel?"

The Judge glared at Humphrey. "Mr Turner, this is highly irregular."

Turning to Donny, the Judge said, "Can you read my lips and under-stand what I'm saying?"

Donny nodded and gave the thumbs-up sign. He pointed at his mouth and moved his left hand in slow circular motions.

The Judge nodded. "Excellent. I take it you can read lips as long as people talk slowly."

Giving the thumbs-up signal, Donny nodded and smiled.

The Judge gestured to the Clerk of Courts. "Please place two chairs in front of the bench for the accused and the security guard, thank you."

The Crown prosecutor and his assistant both smirked, pleased that Humphrey had got off to a bad start.

But I was impressed by the way Donny handled himself. Even with all your faculties, a courtroom is a scary place to be.

After everyone was seated Humphrey stood up and addressed the Jury.

Hoping for some sympathy for the defendant, he said: "Gentlemen of the Jury, in response to the Prosecutor's assertions, I state categor-ically, my client is not guilty and the evidence is only circumstantial. I want you to understand that he comes from a very disadvantaged background and has profound disabilities.

"Donny Buckle was born on Tarakine Pastoral Station in the Western Queensland Channel country in the late 1950s. He was a premature baby with hearing loss and Aphasia, which is the inability to formulate language because of damage to the speech part of his brain.

"Abandoned by his family, he was rescued by a couple of Christian missionaries and taken to an Aboriginal mission until the age of fifteen. Needing more help with sign language and lip-reading, he was fostered by Pastor Carey's family seven years ago."

As Humphrey sits down, the judge clears his throat, "A-hem! Thank you, Mr Turner. I will allow the Prosecutor to restate his opening address to the Jury and the Defendant."

The Crown Prosecutor restated his opening submission and Donny, who'd been calm before this, became agitated and shook his head 'no' a couple of times.

When the Crown Prosecutor finished his opening address, he said, "May it please your Honour, I wish to call the accused to the witness box."

Donny took the Oath by placing his hand on the Bible, was allowed just to nod rather than recite the Oath and then was led to the witness box.

The Crown Prosecutor rose to his feet. His attention still focused on his papers. He straightened up, looked at Donny and asked, "Can you explain to the court, in your own words, Oh, I mean in sign language, what you did on the day in question?"

Donny looked up at the ceiling and gestured with his hands as if conversing with God. Holding his left hand down, he moved his index and middle finger back and forth as if walking. He followed this by moving his arms in a swimming action.

The Prosecutor responded with a smile and confirmed, "For the benefit of the Jury, I take it you thought it was a nice day. You decided to walk out to Six Mile Creek and go for a swim. Is that correct?"

Donny gave the thumbs-up sign.

Some of the jurors chuckled as they warmed to Donny's childlike manner and antics.

The Prosecutor also smiled. "Good. Tell me what you did when you got to Six Mile Creek."

Donny put his open hand above his eyes, shading them. He then moved his head around as if looking for something. He drew an outline of a person and shook his head 'no', pretending to unbutton his shirt.

The Prosecutor nodded. "I'm sure everyone understood that.

But for the benefit of the jury, please nod if you agree that you looked around to make sure nobody was there. That when you were satisfied no one was there you proceeded to remove your clothing to swim. Is that correct?"

Donny responded with thumbs-up.

"What happened next?" the Prosecutor asked.

Donny moved his arms in a swimming motion and pointed left and right.

"Okay," said the Prosecutor. "You swam up and down the creek and then you got out of the water and put on your clothes."

The Judge interrupted with an irritated tone. "Mr Chaney, you are leading the accused. Please allow him to tell his own story and you can confirm our understanding of it."

The Prosecutor's usually jovial face turned to stone as he replied, "My apologies your Honour. It's an unusual situation I find myself in; it is difficult not to provide assistance."

The Judge wanting the last word said, "I think the accused is quite capable of making himself understood without your help."

The Prosecutor nodded to the Judge, turned back to Donny, saying, "Okay Donny, continue please."

Donny moved his arms in a swimming motion for a second or so, stopped, then made a hand gesture like someone throwing something.

I knew exactly what that was: Kurt throwing the rock after Scooter had gone off to steal Donny's clothes.

Donny moved his left arm in a long arc as if tracing a rainbow and at one end of the arc both hands came together in a loud clap. He then threw his hands up into the air like an explosion.

The Prosecutor frowned. "You're trying to tell the court that someone else was there and threw something at you, and it hit the water next to you?"

With a thumbs-up sign, Donny nodded and smiled.

The Prosecutor paused for a moment, deep in thought. With a serious look on his face, he said: "I am going to make this as clear as I can.

"Earlier, you told the court that when you arrived, you looked around and nobody was there. In fact, you checked first before you removed your clothing. Now you are telling me that someone threw something at you. I submit that nobody was there. That you made this up because you want to blame someone else."

Donny jumped to his feet, furiously shaking his head 'no' and tightly clenching his fists. He uttered a strange guttural sound, trying to speak.

The guard jumped up, took hold of Donny and forced him to sit down. I noticed the Prosecutor now had a satisfied, smug look on his face.

The shock tactics appeared to have worked, judging by the startled looks on the Jurors' faces.

My stomach was in knots. I knew Donny was telling the truth. Silently, I asked: Why isn't Humphrey doing something? But he just stared at his papers on the bench.

The Judge then picked up his wooden hammer – it's called a gavel – and banged it twice, "The court will adjourn for a short twenty-minute break for the defendant to calm down.

The Bailiff stood. "All rise," he ordered, as the Judge left the chamber.

I got up and headed for the toilets.

No one was in there except me. Feeling apprehensive and nervous, I had a pee then decided to take a seat in a cubicle.

I'd just closed the cubicle door when I heard the toilet door open. There was a sound of shuffling feet and the toilet door opened again. I heard a familiar voice. It was Humphrey. "Good morning, Your Honour," he said. "What are you doing in the Public facilities?"

The Judge replied: "No need for formality in here, Humphrey. To answer your question, a plumber's working on my Chambers' toilet because it's backed up – just like my long list of cases."

Humphrey grunted, "Oh," as the sound of running water told me he was washing his hands.

The Judge asked, "By the way, why didn't you have an interpreter today?"

"I did," said Humphrey. "But she called in sick this morning and the agency had no one else available."

The Judge told Humphrey, "Between you and me, while your client seems to understand the proceedings, I nearly called off today's hearing. But I was selfishly reminded that after this case I promised to take my wife on holiday. A delay would have caused me to break that promise. I've done that too many times before and I committed to myself not to do it this time."

"Your secret is safe with me," said Humphrey. "Happy wife, happy life."

I heard the Judge open the toilet door and say, "Yes, you understand."

I stayed in the cubicle until I was sure I was alone again.

Back in court, the Prosecutor quizzed Donny: "Tell the court what happened after this alleged missile was thrown."

Donny blinked a couple of times, raised an open hand as if shading his eyes and moved his head from side to side. Then he used both arms in a swimming motion, followed by two fingers in a walking motion. Wary of the guard by his side, he slowly stood up.
Pretending to slip his pants on, he pulled at the front of his shirt, put one hand over his eyes, and looked around with a worried look on his face.

The Prosecutor rose to his feet. "So, I take it you looked up, swam to the bank of the creek and put your trousers back on. But you allege that your shirt was nowhere to be seen. What did you do then?"

Donny shaded his eyes again and looked around. Then with one hand drew a circle and with the other hand used two fingers as if walking away.

Still standing, the Prosecutor confirmed, "You claim you looked for your shirt and unable to find it, you walked back into town. However, you never made it back into town, did you?"

Donny shook his head 'no'.

The Prosecutor's voice became excited. "That's right. The police picked you up on the main road, minus your shirt. They were responding to a call about the assault at the swimming hole.

"There is quite a time gap between when you left the swimming hole and when the police found you. Please tell the court what you did during that period."

Donny didn't respond but looked around as if wanting assistance. He cupped his hand to his right ear and shrugged.

The Prosecutor apologised. "I'm sorry, I'm going too fast," and repeated the statement more slowly.

Donny shrugged again, used his fingers to walk and raised his forearm over his eyes, like a 'damsel in distress' in a silent movie.

Adjusting his wig, the Prosecutor said, "So you want us to believe you were upset and just wandered around?

"Well, I submit you did more than just wander around. In fact, it will be alleged that when you encountered the victim, you placed your blue shirt over her head to disable her and prevent her from identifying you.

"That's why you did not have a shirt. And that's why you can't account for the time between the assault and when the police found you."

Donny became wild-eyed. He violently shook his head and made pitiful guttural sounds as if trying to say 'no'. He clenched his fists again, thumped them hard on the chair's armrests, but remained seated this time.

The Judge picked up his Gavel, banged it twice on the desk calling a halt to the proceedings. He announced, "The Court shall adjourn for the day."

The Clerk of the Court stood up. "All rise for your Honour," he shouted.

We all stood as the Judge swiftly left the Chamber.

I sat down again with my eyes fixed on Donny while he was led out of the courtroom.

I felt sick in the guts 'cos I knew Scooter had been trying to pinch Donny's clothes. He only got his blue shirt. But I didn't know what happened after that. Was it Donny, or could it have been Scooter who assaulted Rachel Carey?

I figured everything was pointing at Scooter. But things weren't looking too flash for Donny, either.

Upon leaving the court, I was hoping he'd get off and that would be the end of the matter.

The youngest member of my audience seems a little restless. "Pete, can we have another drink," he asks. "Then can you tell me more about the court case?"

"Well Josh, I can't really. I was only allowed two days off from school to attend it. But there were more lessons to learn from the experience."

The next day I went in and found the public gallery closed. I asked someone in the corridor what was going on. They directed me to an office. I nervously went in and behind the counter was this old guy. He said, "G'day son, what can I do for you?"

"I came all the way from Pomona to sit in on a court case, but they said the public gallery is closed."

The old guy leaned over the counter, peering at me. "Which case are you interested in?"

I turned and pointed out the door, "The Donny Buckle one."

"Ahh, Courtroom One," he said. "They're hearing the victim's evidence in Courtroom One today, so it's a closed court.

"Sorry, mate, looks like a wasted journey. Why were you interested in that case?"

"I am doing a school project on Democracy in Action and wanted to do it on the Jury system."

The old guy said, "That's a shame. We have no other Jury cases on today." He pointed to a display of brochures on his counter. "The best I can do is to give you a brochure on what a Juror needs to know. Here, take one of these."

I never got to go back and hear the rest of the case against Donny. Later, I heard he was found guilty of the assault. He got nine years but would be out in five if he behaved himself.

Knowing Donny was in prison gave me quite a few bad nights. I felt guilty that I hadn't spoken up. But after a while, I convinced myself that the police must've had more evidence.

Josh pipes up, "Yeah, maybe they got DNA evidence on him?"

I laugh as I explain to Josh, "They didn't have that technology in the late Seventies. You know, Josh, I kept on thinking I should have said something. The longer I held back, the harder it got to put my hand up. Time passed quickly; lots happened. Things were said and done that couldn't be changed.

"I wish now I could have been man enough to speak up and turn back the clock. That's something for you to think about, eh Josh?

"Okay, let's have a spell and that drink."

A cool sea breeze wafts through the house; drinks in hand, we move to the verandah where we can take full advantage of it.

While we are settling into our chairs, Josh asks, "What about Kate's part of the story; we've heard nothing about her side of your story."

"Patience, my dear cousin, I was coming to that.

"Kate, would you mind telling Josh how a big-time lawyer like you came to be at Pomona, and go from there?"

"Sure," laughs Kate.

"I have to admit, when I decided to become a lawyer, I had very naïve ideas about justice for all.

"I worked hard and became a partner of a well-known firm.

"We had several big companies as clients. It was a ruthless business. I defended many people who weren't very honest and used the system to their advantage. All along, I had high ideals and remained passionate about the law providing a level playing field.

"It played on my mind that some of my clients were dodgy. They had lots of money, so the little guy always missed out.

"To keep my sanity, I decided to turn my back on the Big Boys and became a Legal Aid lawyer, helping those in most need. It didn't pay as well, but at least I could sleep at night.

"That's how I ended up at Pomona, working for the Community Advocates Centre and, Josh, it's where I'm going to start my part of the story."

Chapter 4
Community Lawyer, Kate

While working as an advocate, I regularly visited those on remand at the Correctional Centre.

One particularly memorable day, I visited an inmate remanded for housebreaking. He was a bit of a wise-guy and when I asked him how he was going to plead he replied.

"With my record, what difference would it make? I've got no bloody chance. Just like that poor black bastard, Donny, who can't hear or talk."

Interested, I asked: "Yeah, what sort of chance do you reckon he had?

"You young lawyers; you're all the same," said my client.

 "You reckon you can change the world. Well, I'm in the real world and I think you're wasting your time on me. Save the deaf-mute if you really want to save someone. I reckon he's the only innocent one in here – wouldn't hurt a fly."

Although I didn't think what he'd said would hold any merit, I asked around at the office about the deaf-mute case.

I was told the case against Donny Buckle was 'open-and-shut'. Out of interest, I decided to get a transcript.

When I asked the Clerk of Court for a copy, he pulled out the transcript and said, "Oh, that's right, The Crown versus Buckle.

"Now there's a case that fits our Lady of Justice, Themis, with her blindfold and scales in hand.

"Buckle, the poor sod had no chance with old Humphrey Turner running the case.

"God! Humphrey hardly knew what day it was, even when he was sober, and never got the deaf-mute an interpreter."

The Clerk of Court's words spurred me on to read through the transcript. But there was nothing in it I could use to call for a retrial. To do that, I would have to present new evidence.

During further discussion about Donny's case with the Clerk of Court, I asked about Humphrey Turner and thought I might have a chat with him.

The Clerk said, "Yeah, I know where old Humphrey is. I wouldn't call it an office though – has a corner table in the Saloon Bar at the Noosa Beach Hotel. He even does some of his Briefs there."

After one of my court appearances in Noosa, I decided to meet Humphrey. I wanted to get his angle and a feel for the case.

As I recall, before pushing on the hotel's Saloon Bar door, I had to pause to summon up the courage to go inside. In those days women were discouraged from going into a saloon bar – it was as if we were desecrating a sacred site.

As the door opened, I cautiously peered into the dimly lit smoke-filled bar. A few heads turned to stare. I can still see those frosty looks; they sent a shiver up my spine. Squaring my shoulders, I marched up to the bar and asked the Barman, "Is Humphrey Turner around?"

As he wiped down the bar top, he nodded towards the far corner and said, "Over there, Miss."

I weaved my way around a few tables while the 'regulars' continued drinking as if they hadn't seen me. At a table with a whiskey glass and a pile of papers on it, sat a big man with a balding head.

"Are you Humphrey Turner," I asked?

He looked surprised. "Who wants to know?"

I held out my hand, "Hi, I'm Kate Maybury, Community Advocate working at Pomona."

Humphrey reached up and lightly held my hand. He didn't shake it, but mumbled, "Ahhh, Pomona, the Roman Goddess of fruit trees."

I sat down opposite Humphrey and asked, "You mean me?"

"No, the name, Pomona."

Nervously, I pulled out a cigarette. Unsure of what reaction I was going to get for the cigarette, or for just being there, I said, "Do you mind?"

Humphrey picked up his whiskey glass as if to propose a toast: "To your poison and mine. So, what brings you here?"

"While I was visiting a client in Boggo Road Gaol, he mentioned Donny Buckle, so I decided to read the trial transcript."

Humphrey's bushy eyebrows flicked up. "Aah, yes. I recall that one. A sad case: pretty much open-and-shut. I think you'll find you're wasting your time, there."

I took a puff of my cigarette and told him I disagreed.

"I'm questioning the fairness of the trial. Without an interpreter, how could Donny understand what was going on?"

Humphrey thumped his empty glass down. Almost shouting, he said, "Since when has life been fair! What has fairness got to do with anything, especially when you're a deaf-mute?

"Well, the Judge and Jury seemed to think it was fair. I did try to get him an interpreter. It wasn't my fault that she rang in sick on the morning of the trial."

I quickly stubbed out my cigarette. "I just hoped to get a feel for the case, Mr Turner. But obviously, I've come at a bad time."

Realising he'd been 'over the top' in his response, Humphrey took a deep breath and sighed. "Please forgive me for my agitation. All I get these days is criticism and zero appreciation. Everyone just abuses the system. No one tells the truth anymore.

"Understand, my learned friend, old wounds may have healed, and the pain gone, but the scars remain.

"I know you're wondering why I'm sitting here indulging in self-pity. I was like you once. I believed passionately in justice and fairness. Look where it got me. But if you want to go off on a crusade, I won't stand in your way. Good day Kate."

I got up from the table and without saying another word left the bar.

There was nothing more I could glean from Humphrey. I had to dig elsewhere. I would start at Boggo Road Gaol. I'd already visited it many times and each time I couldn't wait to leave. It was old, outdated and depressing.

I shall never forget my first meeting with Donny, how his eyes lit up with joy at the sight of me. He pointed at me, held up three fingers and counted them.

I did the same and said, "Donny, are you saying that since you've been in here you've only had three visitors?"

Donny nodded. His expression changed to one of sadness, his top lip quivered, and he bowed his head. After a few seconds, he lifted his head and our eyes met. He was welling up with tears, and so was I. Almost in unison, we brushed them away.

He made a sign with one finger, pretended to put something in each ear and placed his hand over his heart. Then he lifted his other hand to his ear. Holding up his hand again, he made a sign with two fingers. Donny stood up and walked around the table in a feminine way placing his index finger next to his ear and made little circles around it.

I smiled at the thought of us playing Charades. "I think you mean a doctor and a crazy woman visited you – right?"

Holding up one finger, he nodded. Then he held up two fingers and shook his head to indicate 'no'.

"Oh, I think I know what you mean. Was the woman a psychologist?"

Donny nodded enthusiastically. He raised three fingers, pointed them at his throat and my white blouse. Then he fashioned a Cross with two fingers, put his hands together in prayer and looked up at the ceiling.

I understood the third person must have been the prison Chaplain. I was shocked. "Donny, are you telling me that no family or friends have visited you?"

Donny's top lip quivered again as he tried to control his emotions. He slumped back in his chair, stared at the table and refused to look at me.

I leaned forward and touched his hand. He looked up. With tears in his eyes, he made guttural sounds, trying to talk. It was a pitiful sight.

He was crying and I was trying to hold back my own tears, without success; had to grab tissues from my handbag for both of us. Lost for words; I could not think of how to comfort him.

This emotional pressure I hadn't expected. I needed a cigarette. I asked if he'd mind if I smoked. He indicated okay. I pulled two cigarettes out of my pack and offered him one, but he waved it away. Then he pointed at me and threw his hands open, in a questioning gesture.

I took it as meaning 'why'?

"Oh, why am I here? I want to talk to you about your case. I want to know in your own words what happened."

Donny rocketed out of his chair, banged his hands on his head. The look of anguish on his face was tragic. Seeing this, the Prison Guard entered, grabbed Donny and began removing him from the Visitors centre.

I jumped up and protested. "No! Please! It's alright!"

The guard led Donny back to the table. Pointing at the chair, he said, "You stay there! If you do that again, the visit's over. Got it?"

Donny gave the thumbs-up sign to the guard.

I sat down again and stubbed out my cigarette. Looking straight at Donny, I asked: "Do you know why you are in prison?"

Donny nodded and pretended to unbutton and remove his shirt. He slowly stood up. He looked nervously at the guard and pretended to unbuckle his trousers. Then he moved his arms rhythmically in 'free- style-swimming' fashion.

I scrunched up my face when I realised what he was suggesting.

"Are you saying that you think you are in here for swimming with no clothes on? Is that what you're saying?"

Donny sat down and smiled with a thumbs-up sign. He waved to get my attention, pretended to unbutton his shirt again and feigned tossing it away. Then he held up his hand in a stopping motion and adjusted a pretend cap. Holding closed fists, he moved them as if driving a car. I leaned forward and grabbed his hands to get his attention.

"I read the transcript of your trial. I think you're telling me about the police picking you up without your shirt. But you're not in here for a nicky-swim. You're here because the Court says you raped a girl at the gorge."

Donny pulled his hand away and banged his fists down hard onto the table. He shook his head furiously. He jumped up and pointed to his pelvis, thrusting his hips back and forth. Then waved his hands 'no'

Two Prison Guards suddenly appeared. They grabbed hold of Donny by the arms to restrain him. One said firmly, "That's enough. I warned you to behave. The visit's over Miss."

Standing up, I watched helplessly as they led Donny away. He glanced back at me with a pleading look. Haunted by that look; it stopped me from sleeping for several nights. I had to take action.

The next day, I paid a visit to Pastor Carey. He was Rachel Carey's father and Donny's foster father. As far as I could tell, the Carey family had given Donny a good family life.

I was a little nervous when I arrived out the front of the Holy Spirit Mission because some of my questions were likely to hit a nerve.

As I parked my car, Pastor Carey's head popped around the open church door.

He stepped forward to greet me as I offered him my hand, saying, "Hi, how are you? I'm Kate Maybury."

The Pastor extended one hand and warmly placed the other hand on top of mine. It was a comforting, fatherly handshake.

"Hello," he said. "May the good Lord be with you, my girl: have we met before?"

I shook my head 'no' and he responded with, "Have you come about our blessed Fete?"

"No, it's nothing like that," I replied. "I'm a lawyer from the Community Advocates Centre and I've come to talk to you about Donny Buckle."

Pastor Carey recoiled. He stood stock-still for a few moments, and then said, "I think you should come inside. I don't wish to discuss this out here."

As he led me through the doorway, he began questioning me. "Why are you trying to dredge things up again? Don't you think our family has been tormented enough?"

I knew that was coming. I was on edge and could have done with a cigarette, but this was not the place to light up.

"I can understand your reaction, Pastor. But the problem is, I don't think he's responsible for the attack. I think he's innocent."

Pastor Carey pointed at me and yelled, "How dare you come into this House of God with this rubbish about *his innocence*?

"Our family gave him a home and he repaid our charity by robbing my daughter of *her innocence*. Whatever you have to say about Donny Buckle, I don't want to hear it."

I took a deep breath before saying, "But Pastor, as a man of God, surely you would agree God's work is in all things, both good and evil. Wouldn't He find it in his heart for truth and justice to shine through, even in the darkest moment?"

Pastor Carey folded his arms defensively and nodded, "You're right about God moving in mysterious ways. I've asked myself the same question about our problem many times.

"Perhaps He has brought you here so I can gain some insight into this mess. Did Donny send you?"

"No, Pastor Carey," I replied. "I read the transcript of the court case. I'm not sure I can explain why, but I've always believed in the importance of justice and fairness for the less fortunate members of our society. Even as a small girl, I had a strong desire to right wrongs, and I could sense when things weren't right.

"I've come to ask your permission to talk with Rachel."

Paster Carey rubbed his chin and thought for a few moments. "I'm not sure you've answered my question. But I am sure about one thing: Rachel isn't ready for what you have to say."

"What makes you think that?"

Pastor Carey shrugged.

"I don't know. I guess our relationship has changed. Since the unfortunate event, trusting people has been difficult for Rachel. I can't see how this could help her."

Wanting to make my point hit home, I raised one hand and held up two fingers. "Firstly, if I'm right, the wrong person is behind bars, which means the real perpetrator is still at large and could strike again."

Pastor Carey looked puzzled. "Hang on: you're telling me that twelve God-fearing people who heard all of the evidence got it wrong. On what basis would you make such a claim?"

My nerves were getting to me. I turned towards the Church door: "Pastor Carey, may we step outside? I need a cigarette. I hope you don't mind?"

He gave me a fatherly look of sympathy and said, "My dear, you're in a house of God. You shouldn't feel nervous. I apologise if I have come over a bit strong. But you must understand it's going to take time for us all to get over this unpleasantness."

We walked to the car park where we continued our conversation as I dived into my handbag and lit up.

"Well, I've met Donny," I said. "I feel he's not responsible for the assault on Rachel and that he was telling the truth about someone else being at the swimming hole. I just don't have the evidence – yet."

Pastor Carey stepped back and turned as if to leave, then spun around. He looked fierce, angry.

Red in the face and pointing at me, he fumed: "How dare you come here with a half-baked story like this? And with no evidence to back up your claim. What am I supposed to think? Well, my mind is made up. I think you should leave right now. I want no more of this nonsense!"

I went over to a bin, stubbed out my cigarette and tried to smooth things over.

"I'm truly sorry, Pastor Carey, for upsetting you. It was never my intention to do that. But I thank you for your time."

He managed to say "Good day" before he stormed off.

After that, I had to take stock and work out what to do next.

Josh takes the cue and says, "Yes. If you couldn't talk to Rachel, how were you going to get to what really happened?"

Kate smiles: "An excellent question, Josh. I decided I needed a different approach and left things to cool down for a few days. Then I hit on a new strategy."

Kate dives back into the story.

It was time for me to summon up a bit more courage and make a small investment.

I returned to the church armed with a huge bag full of new stuffed toys as donations for the church fete. Taking a deep breath before stepping into the church, I saw a couple of helpers and Pastor Carey going through cardboard boxes of donated items.

He looked up and smiled. "Hi Kate," he said. "Your donations I'll accept, but not your wild theories."

I handed over the bag and asked, "Look, is there somewhere private we can talk?"

The Pastor pointed to a side room, and we left his helpers sorting items on the floor. He ushered me into a kitchen area. As he closed the door, I took the opportunity to talk first.

"Last time we met I told you I had two things to say," I reminded him.

"The second thing I was going to say is that I know what Rachel is going through. I know how she's feeling."

Pastor Carey turned around. Scratching his balding head, he eyed me quizzically. "How could you possibly know?"

I had to tell him my shocking secret right then because I wanted to help Rachel and Donny too.

I said: "I know because I've been there."

The Pastor looked at me as if he didn't get my meaning.

I explained: "Pastor Carey, as a very young girl, I was the subject of sexual abuse by a so-called family friend. Since then, I've been nervous around older men. It's one of the reasons I resigned as a partner in a large City law firm and came out here to practise Community Law."

Pastor Carey's jaw dropped.

For a second or two, he was quiet. Then he said, "My girl, I can tell it's a difficult thing for you to talk about.

"Maybe I've been too hasty. Why don't we go to the Tea Rooms and discuss this over a cup of tea? It will give me a chance to think through what's best for Rachel. I'm still very protective of her fragile state, so I need to question whether you're the right person to help her."

We walked over to the Pomona Tea Rooms and placed our order.

After the waitress left, I glanced up at Pastor Carey and said, "Rachel will be going through different emotional stages. I did too.

"Firstly, I denied it happened and refused to think about it or discuss it. Later, when I realised it had changed me and it wasn't going to go away, I was angry. I wasn't a bad person, so why me?

"Then sadness took over because I felt some part of me had been taken away and it was never coming back.

"In the end, I had to channel the hurt into something positive; otherwise, it would have destroyed me.

"That's why I became a lawyer. But the damage managed to continue getting in the way.

"As I said earlier, I've always wanted to see justice and fairness done. Instead, I found those virtues corrupted by people in the corporate world whose only motivation was money and, ultimately, the power it wields. Disillusioned but not defeated, I realised that my path lay with helping those who don't have the money or the knowledge to fight for justice."

Pastor Carey patted my hand in a kindly manner. "Well, my dear, in that we have something in common. You fight for people's rights, and I fight to save their souls.

"While you've been talking, I've realised I haven't been able to get close to Rachel since the assault. Now I know why. It's the old Rachel I've been trying to find. Her view of the world is different now. Why did I not recognise this?

"Perhaps you will be able to reach her, whereas I can't. So, I will trust you and pray I'm doing the right thing here.

"Kate, I'm saying I have no objections to you talking with her."

I was relieved. "Thank you, Pastor Carey," I said. "It would be wonderful if some good could come out of my own experience. I will do my best to help Rachel."

He gulped down the last of his tea, then asked: "Kate, would you mind if I mention your situation to Rachel? She's lost her trust in people and shut herself off emotionally. Telling her that you went through the same trauma might convince her to meet with you."

Chapter 5
Meeting Rachel

I waited several days before the phone call came.

Pastor Carey arranged for me to meet Rachel while he took the rest of the family out for a picnic.

They decided she'd be more comfortable and feel safer at home.

At this crucial point in the story, my phone pings: it's a message from Josh's Mum.

"Sorry Kate, I just got a text message from Aunt Barbara. It's almost dinnertime. She wants Josh home. I think it's time to call stumps. You probably need to go home too. We'll, have to finish this another day."

Josh protests loudly. "No way, Big Cuz!

"I want to hear the rest of it. Can't we have dinner with you? Can we have pizza then you don't have to cook? Come on, Pete. Can we?"

"Okay then. That sounds like a great idea. But what about you, Kate, can you stay?"

"I don't mind if it means I get out of cooking. I'll have to ring Hubby so he and Brodie can fend for themselves."

I quickly text Aunt Barbara, saying Josh can stay for pizza and if Roxy wants, she can join us too.

I place the order and we decide we'll wait for Roxy before continuing the story.

We are out the front on the verandah when Roxy arrives. As the sun is setting, we decide to retreat inside.

Getting comfy on one of my big chairs, Kate adjusts the cushion behind her and continues.

I was surprised at how nervous I felt the day I knocked on the Pastor's front door. Yet I should have expected it: I would be facing my own fears again, opening old wounds. But I hoped it would be worth it if I could help Rachel and at the same time ensure justice was done.

After knocking a few times, there was no response. I wondered if Rachel was hiding from me. As I turned to leave, a slight noise made me stop.

The door had opened, just a crack. I heard a soft voice say, "Are you, Kate?"

"Yes. I'm looking for Rachel."

The door opened wider. "Sorry I didn't answer straight away. I was resting out the back. I'm Rachel."

"Hi Rachel, it's nice to meet you."

There was an awkward pause as we stared at each other, so I asked, "Rachel, do you mind if I come in?"

Rachel pulled back the door. "Sorry, I'm still half asleep. Actually, could we go for a walk instead? I need to clear my head."

"No, not at all. It's a beaut day for a walk. Don't you agree?"

Rachel nodded, locked the door, and followed me down the pathway.

"I need to get out, I'm climbing the walls and my parents won't let me out of their sight," she said. "I don't want to go into town though, so can we go this way?"

As she joined me, I pointed left to affirm her choice. She nodded and said, "It's... it's just that I still feel funny around people.

"I know what they're saying. Some are so rude. They stare through me like... like I'm not there. I hate it."

Glancing at her pretty young face, I sympathised. "Yes, I know. Ignorant people can be very cruel."

Rachel gave me a searching look as if trying to decide if I could be trusted.

"My Dad thinks you might be able to help me. He said that you would know what I'm going through. Are you a Counsellor?"

"No. I'm a lawyer with the Community Advocates Centre. However, I'm going to tell you something about me.

"When I was a little girl of about five a close family friend assaulted me. As I grew older, I could see how life could be unfair and unjust. I decided to channel my anger into something useful. I became a lawyer to support people seeking fairness and justice."

We'd reached a fork in the path. "Rachel, shall we go down along this lane to the river?"

Rachel's mood seemed to have brightened, although we'd only walked a short way. She said, "Yes, that's a great idea. I haven't been down there for ages – you know since *it* happened."

I placed my hand on Rachel's arm. "I did that too, avoided places and people for a while. Everything I did was affected by the events of that fateful day. I had to learn it didn't have to control who I was or where I was going. It was only one event in my life and carried no more weight than any other difficult event.

"All I'm saying is, don't put anything you are planning to do in the same sentence as 'on that day it happened'… et cetera."

Rachel grimaced and gritted her teeth.

"But Kate, it's so hard. It makes me so angry and sad at the same time. Angry, because Donny lived with us, and I treated him like my brother. Sad, because I trusted him and now I don't trust anyone.

"I didn't know what was going to happen. I thought maybe I was going to die. But what upsets me the most is that I… I wanted the first time to be with the guy I love and now that's all been taken away from me."

I could feel her turmoil. Like me, Rachel had been cheated of something precious.

I put a reassuring hand on her back and gave it what I hoped was a comforting rub, saying, "That's good Rachel, to have those feelings and be able to talk about it openly."

She shaded her eyes as she glanced back at me and asked, "Why Kate?"

"It means you're not blocking your feelings, and you know why you feel that way."

Rachel looked at me closely: "What sort of things did you go through?"

I thought for a moment as I wanted to choose my words carefully.

"Although I was too young to understand, I went through different phases.

"At first, I wanted to believe it hadn't happened. Then when I told my family about it, I was not believed. They decided I was making it up and I was made to feel ashamed because of the drama I'd caused for them, even though none of it was my fault.

"I became angry and kept asking myself, why me? The sadness I felt was extraordinary; everything around me seemed to have changed. Finally, I discovered nothing around me had changed. It was me who had changed."

Rachel pointed at the water and exclaimed, "Kate, look, there's fish jumping. I love nature. I love being outdoors. It makes me feel closer to God."

This told me her *nudie* swimming may have been her way of innocently indulging in one of nature's gifts.

I gently took Rachel's arm and guided her to a fallen log.

"Why don't we sit on this log and just take everything in? Being in nature does lift the spirits, doesn't it?"

We sat quietly for a while as a soft breeze brushed the heads of the reeds in a wave-like motion. Light from the sun danced on the water.

Small birds darted about chasing each other. Occasionally, a series of rings would appear on the still water, where a fish had surfaced to chase an insect. However, the quietness didn't last long. A group of children appeared, running along with their dog. The children were laughing, and the dog was barking loudly.

Rachel was watching them. I could tell she was envious. I'd experienced the same type of envy many times after I'd been attacked. She was most likely thinking they're so carefree and innocent – if they only knew.

Rachel asked, "Kate, can we go on further down the river?"

"Sure," I said, and we both stood, stretching a bit before setting out along the path.

I noticed Rachel wanted to take the walk but there was something hesitant in her step. "Rachel, what's troubling you right now?" I asked.

"I'm wondering why you've come to see me. You're not a Counsellor, so is it something to do with my case because one of Dad's friends reckoned I could get compensation? I don't want to go through everything again, just to get some money."

I had to take a deep breath before responding.

"Rachel, before we move on, I need to be honest with you. I've read the transcript of your case. There are aspects of it that are disturbing."

Rachel broke away from me. She was angry. I caught up with her.

As I reached her side she burst out, "Kate I don't care! 'Cos if Donny had done the right thing and said he was guilty I wouldn't have had to face all those strangers. It was so embarrassing, answering all the questions the Prosecutor asked me. And you know what the most traumatic thing was? I could tell the Jurors just weren't interested. Two were asleep and another one was yawning."

"Rachel, I have to ask you this. Do you know for sure it was Donny who attacked you? Because if he didn't, the real offender is still at large and could strike again."

Rachel stopped dead in her tracks. "What! You can't be serious. The Court said he was guilty." She held up the palm of her hand and waved. "End of story."

"But Rachel, we both know that is not the end of the story. We've both been through this and it can never be the end. It's always going to crop up. A person acting strangely, a wrong word said – something in the paper or on the news."

Rachel stared out over the water; she had tears in her eyes. I hugged her.

"You're upset; I'm so sorry. I'll walk you back home. I won't press you anymore. I'll give you my phone number. You can call me anytime."

Rachel brushed the tears from her cheeks with each hand.

"Thanks, Kate. Thanks for being totally honest with me. Everyone seems so fake these days."

Recalling Rachel's experience causes Kate to pause in her storytelling. I notice her swallowing hard and clearing her throat. No tears that I can see, though.

I ask her if she'd like a drink of water, and she nods. While I'm getting it, I hear Roxy comment: "Boy, that part was real e-mo stuff. But guys are always giving us girls a hard time. The world would be a better place without men."

Josh jumps up, grabs hold of Roxy's arms, attempting to wrestle her. "Get off the grass, Sis," he says. "What guy would want you anyway?"

Roxy retorts, "Well, you're touching me." Josh quickly lets go. "Errrr, I've got Roxy germs!. I'm gonna die." He drops to the floor, rolls over, and grabs his throat, "Ahhhhh."

Handing Kate the glass of water, I tackle the duelling youngsters, "Okay, that's enough out of you two. Do you want us to continue this story or not?"

"Yeah! Shoosh, Josh, I want to hear more," says Roxy.

Josh throws a cushion at Roxy and hisses, "Shoosh yourself."

She keeps the cushion, which annoys Josh so he pulls an ugly face.

Just then there's a knock at the door. Josh yells at the top of his voice, "PIZZA!"

I look at Kate and say, "Just in time, these two are getting restless."

The pizza's devoured at warp speed.

Keen to hear more of the story, Roxy asks: "Did you get to talk to Rachel again?"

Kate empties her glass, dabs her lips with a paper napkin before answering, "I was coming to that before you two went ballistic. Here's what happened next."

A couple of weeks later Rachel called me and we agreed to meet at the Tea Rooms.

I was pacing up and down outside thinking she wasn't going to show, when I felt a soft tap on my shoulder. Rachel had snuck up on me. She was on edge and quite shaky.

What a brave girl she is, I thought. If she'd been a little less nervous, I would have given her a high five.

"Oh Rachel, well done," I said. "For a few moments there, I thought you might not be coming."

"No way; I came a little late because I just didn't want to be left standing out here on my own."

I nodded. "Perfectly understandable, young lady. So glad to see you. Let's go in."

We went into the Tea Rooms and sat at a table near the door.

Looking around, I noticed the long stares and some whispering.

Rachel saw this too. Leaning across the table, she said softly, "See what I mean?"

I smiled. "Watch this."

I turned around and glared at an old lady who was blatantly staring. She quickly looked down at her teacup and put it to her lips. Other offenders faked an uninterested look.

"See Rachel, nothing to fear. Let's order."

Rachel smiled nervously and nodded.

A waitress came over to our table and said, "Hey Rach, how-ya going?"

Rachel smiled back. "Hi Kirsty, I'm good. Still got those home-made scones?"

"Yep, sure do; and same for your friend?"

I nodded and waited until the waitress left before saying, "I see you've changed since our last visit. You're much more relaxed."

Rachel lowered her eyes. "Do you think so? Well, I've had time to think a lot and you're right, I have to get on with my life.

"I can't change what happened and I can't change what people think. What I can change are my own feelings. I thought about how things must've been for you, and you were so young. Then I realised I'm older; if you dealt with all that stuff, so can I."

It was such a relief to hear this. I leaned over and patted Rachel's hand in encouragement. "That's wonderful Rachel, you're on the mend now," I said.

Rachel leaned across the table to whisper, "I've been thinking about Donny. Part of me wants to believe it wasn't him. I didn't want to say that in the court, because everyone kept telling me there was overwhelming evidence."

Sitting back in my chair, I said, "Okay. When we're done, why don't we go over to my office? No radar-ears there."

While we were walking across to my office Rachel asked, "Is it fun, being a lawyer?"

I laughed. I'd never considered it a fun job. For me, it was something I had to do.

"Sometimes being a lawyer can be like beating your head against a brick wall; sometimes it makes no sense at all. Then you manage to help someone and see how it changes their life. That's when you realise why you're doing the job."

I ushered Rachel into my office. She glanced around at all the files and papers stacked in neat piles on the desk, on the floor and the filing cabinets. Even the guest chairs had stacks of files on them. All horizontal surfaces that could take a stack of papers were occupied.

Removing one of those stacks off the client's chair in front of my desk, I said, "So sorry Rachel, let me shift these.

"The problem here is that we're so short of funds all the time, there's no money to properly store our files or get extra secretarial help when it's needed."

I sat behind my desk, facing Rachel. Selecting a folder from the files I'd just moved, I said, "In this folder, I have the transcript of the case. I've been over it a couple of times.

"I know this is hard, but do you remember anything that you didn't mention at the trial?"

Rachel sat back, and after a few seconds of reflection said, "Kate, I know you're trying to help. But you and everybody else don't understand.

"There I am, one minute so happy and connected to nature. Then, suddenly everything goes dark and I'm like fighting for my life. I sort of felt as if I'd left my body; it's hard to remember anything now."

I closed the file and responded, "You said at the trial the person who attacked you didn't say anything. Are you sure they didn't say *anything*?"

Rachel put her head in her hands, closed her eyes and whispered, "The only sounds I heard were heavy breathing and grunting. I don't think I'll forget those horrible sounds, ever."

Rachel's shoulders shuddered. She lowered her hands and said, "It makes me go cold just thinking about it, again."

I patted the file on the desk, saying: "Well, that evidence points to Donny. But it doesn't necessarily mean it was him. You never actually saw him, did you?"

Rachel squirmed in the chair, very agitated, she said: "No. Kate, I don't think I can help you. There's nothing more I can tell you."

She was distressed. I had to ease up.

"That's okay Rachel," I answered.

"I had to ask you those questions; in case there was something missing in the transcript. If you think of anything at all, please call me, won't you?"

Rachel stood up to leave. "Of course I will, Kate," she said.

I walked her to the door and watched as she stepped across the road and skipped up the gutter.

In my lounge room, Kate stands and plumps up the big cushion on her chair before settling into it again.

Josh asks, "So what happens now, Kate? It sounds as if you've come to a full stop with Rachel again."

"Well, Josh, this could have been the end of the story, but I came up with a couple of ideas that resulted in some new leads. And you'll soon learn how Pete got involved."

"Yes, Josh," I say. "Kate met up with the Police Sergeant who arrested Donny and that led to some more digging."

Kate nods, "That's true Pete. Meeting the Sergeant is what inspired me to dig deeper. That and my instinct kept the case teasing at my mind. Let me get back to it."

Despite Rachel leaving me in the lurch, so to speak, my hunch about Donny's innocence haunted me.

A couple of weeks later, I was representing a client on a case in which the police officer who'd arrested Donny, Sergeant Collis, was giving evidence.

After the case was adjourned, he and I had a lively discussion about justice and do-gooders. It was my chance to ask him about Donny Buckle's case.

We were outside the courtroom, sitting beside a garden on a low retaining wall.

I asked Sergeant Collis, "I've read the transcript and I'm wondering what you thought of the case?"

"Please call me Mike, we're not in court now," he said. "Anyway, you're wasting your time bringing that one up – an open-and-shut case.

"I caught the dumb beggar without his shirt. It was his shirt that was used in the attack.

"Him claiming someone else was there is all bullshit, and the jury agreed with me – end of story. What's your interest, anyway?"

I was so sick of hearing that 'end-of-story' phrase; and 'open-and-shut' case', I wanted to reach for a bucket and heave! Instead, I held my ground.

"I've met him, and I have the feeling it wasn't him."

Sergeant Collis smiled broadly. "There we go again, another do-gooder. You're wasting your time on the likes of him.

"You lawyers always reckon your client's innocent. The jails are full of them. Doesn't that tell you something?"

"Well Mike, I agree with you on that point. I had a similar discussion with a prisoner at Boggo Road Gaol.

"Just as a matter of interest, before Donny's case, had there been any prior sexual assaults in the same area?"

Tilting his head to one side, Mike looked off into the distance; then he said, "Oh Yes. There were a couple, quite some time ago, but nothing recent and those cases were solved."

Having almost run out of angles and getting only negative answers, I chanced another question: "One more thing, Mike, were there any reports of strange happenings at the swimming hole around the time Rachel Carey was attacked – that you know of?"

Sergeant Collis stood up, leaned with one hand on the wall, "Nah, it's been pretty quiet around these parts. So quiet, HQ is reviewing the Station's status.

"The only event that sticks in my mind happened a few months after Rachel Carey was assaulted.

"This kid, Gordon something, well everyone called him Scooter, hanged himself at the Gorge. Poor kid was one of those Mongoloid kids."

I cringe when I hear that label being used so I corrected him: "You mean he had Down's syndrome."

Sergeant Collis straightened up, lifted his hand off the wall and waved it as he retorted, "Whatever. Anyway, he had a crap upbringing. His mother was a druggie. Didn't know who the father was and when she ended up in the 'nut-house', the grandmother took him in."

Then I asked, "Did the kid leave any kind of note or anything to suggest why he might have done that?"

"Nah, we didn't find anything."

Sergeant Collis glanced at his watch. "Jesus! Look at the time. I'd like to keep chatting, but I got to go."

I slid down from the retaining wall and blocked his path. "Mike, just one more very quick question, please. Do you know the grandmother and where she lives?"

The Sergeant changed the files under one arm to the other as he said, "Don't know her name, but she lives at the caravan park. Just ask anyone there about the old lady and the funny kid with red hair, they'll know."

I shook his hand. "Mike, thanks for your time."

He beamed at me, "My pleasure Kate."

Watching him walk away, my mind was made up. I was convinced something was not right about this case.

I decided I'd visit Scooter's grandmother straight away. There was only one caravan park in the town, so I figured she'd be easy to find.

When I arrived at the caravan park, I spotted a gardener mowing the lawn. I walked over to him and shouted, "Hi there. I'm looking for someone."

He got off the ride-on mower, shaded his eyes and removed his ear- muffs. "Sorry lady, what'd ya say?"

The mower was still going, so I had to shout again, "I'm looking for someone who lives in this caravan park, but I don't know her name. She's an elderly lady; she had a boy called Gordon, who's dead now."

"Oh, you mean Scooter," he said. "Yeah, terrible tragedy. I feel so sorry for Beryl, her family problems and all. She lives over there in that caravan. But she's in town right now. You'll have to come back later."

I was due in court that afternoon, so I returned the next day.

Luckily, I found the elderly lady, Beryl, sitting next to the caravan under a big gum tree. She was reading a book as I approached her.

"Hello there, are you, Beryl? My name's Kate. Lovely day, isn't it?"

Beryl looked up. "Harry said someone was looking for me. Well, you've found me. What's your business, lass? Can't you see I'm busy?"

Her directness stunned me, and I hesitated before saying, "Well I've come to ask you some questions about Gordon?"

She closed her book and stared straight up at me, "Why. Are you from Welfare?"

Feeling awkward and towering over her, I sat down on the grass.

"No. I'm interested in finding out the names of Gordon's friends and the school he went to, stuff like that."

Beryl gripped her book with both hands. "Strange you are asking because nobody else has taken an interest since he died. Not one person has said anything to me since the funeral. Like the poor little *Blighter* never existed.

I just hope he's happy wherever he is. He certainly was short-changed in this life. I told Missie – that's my daughter, not to mess with the druggies. But she never listened. And I told Gordon not to muck around with that Kurt Hoganhoffer. But no, he never took any notice."

I interrupted her. "You mean the Hoganhoffers who own the big dairy?"

She nodded with a long slow head movement, "Oh yeah, and just about everything else in town.

"I'll tell you one thing, despite Gordon drawing the short straw in life, he was a happy-go-lucky kid. But for a while before he died, he changed. He became withdrawn, stayed in the annex a lot, and wouldn't tell me anything.

"Used to eat like a horse but in the days just before he ended his life, he hardly ate anything off his plate."

I then asked, "Did Gordon have any other friends?"

Beryl sat up straight in her camping chair, "Actually, now that you mention it, there was a new kid who used to hang around with Gordon and that Hoganhoffer boy, but I don't know his name. They all went to Pomona High, so the school kids should know."

Getting up from the grass, I said, "Well it's been nice talking to you, Beryl. Maybe we'll meet again."

Beryl picked up her book again and sighed, "I won't hold my breath."

Chapter 6
Meeting Kurt

A few days later, I went over to Pomona High School at siren-time and asked a group of students to point out Kurt.

One of them shouted, "Hey Kurt! Some lady wants to talk to you."

He pointed in my direction. Kurt was at the school gate so, I ushered him to one side. I shook his hand and said, "Hi Kurt. I'm Kate Maybury. I'm a lawyer with the Community Advocates Centre and I've reviewed the Coroner's case on your friend Gordon. I want to ask you a couple of questions."

Kurt's relaxed look changed to one of concern. His stance stiffened, which told me he was anxious.

"You mean my mate Scooter? What if I don't want to answer any of your questions?"

Looking directly into Kurt's eyes, I said, "That's okay because I can easily get the information I want from Pete Gannon. He's Scooter's and your friend, isn't he?"

Kurt straightened up and cheekily replied, "More than that – they're both my Blood Brothers. So I won't have you going around bagging them. My Dad will fix you if you do that."

"I'm not here to tarnish their reputations, only to get the truth," I told him.

Kurt looked angry. "Well, I'll tell you what the truth is. I found poor

Scooter hanging, and it will be with me for the rest of my days. I don't need you to be hanging around, dragging it all back up again."

I dug a bit more: "Was Scooter closer to you or Pete?"

Kurt screwed his face up. "What a strange question. I told you we're Bloods. But since you ask, Pete only became a Blood Brother after I saved his life at the Gorge."

Surprised, I remarked, "Wow. You did that. What happened?"

His attitude changed immediately. "I was down there mucking around and heard someone coming. I hid in the bush behind a rock ledge. It was Pete, but we weren't friends then. He changed into his swimming togs. While he was looking over the edge at the water, I bounced a rock onto the ledge to see what he would do. Stupid bugger spun around, lost his balance, and slipped off. He did the biggest belly flop ever. Then I saw him floating face down. So I jumped in and pulled him out."

I smiled. "You like stirring people up, don't you?"

Kurt smiled back, "Sometimes. Otherwise, everything's boring."

I nodded, "Yes, your right. This place can be boring."

Kurt relaxed his stance and said, "Look lady, I have to go. Maybe you'd like to come and have a look around our dairy some time?"

"Thanks Kurt, I'd love to do that," I replied.

After he left, I went up to two schoolteachers in the schoolyard. "Hi I'm Kate Maybury," I said.

The older teacher had her arms folded. She replied, "Ah-ha, the Community Lawyer; should we be concerned?"

I held out my hand. "No, this is a friendly visit."

The older teacher shook my hand. "Well then," she said. "I'm Mrs Eddy the deputy principal here and this is Mandy Clark, our special-needs assistant."

Mandy and I shook hands. She was one of the people I needed to speak with about Gordon.

"I've just been going over a couple of local cases," I said.

"One involved a Down's syndrome lad called Gordon, or Scooter. I was wondering what he was like?"

Mandy grimaced. "Oh, poor Scooter! I'll never understand what could have driven him to do such a thing.

"He is… I mean… he was such a happy-go-lucky boy, despite his problems. He loved coming to school, even though he could barely write his name, let alone construct a whole sentence."

"Mandy, did Scooter have lots of friends?"

She thought for a moment and shook her head 'no'.

"He didn't mix much. But strangely enough the son of the owner of the local dairy…" I interrupted her: "You mean Kurt?"

"Yes, that's the boy.

"Well, he took Scooter under his wing and watched out for him."

I asked, "Do you know Pete Gannon? He used to knock around with them too, according to Kurt."

Mandy looked at Mrs Eddy and shook her head.

"I know very little about Pete. He's new to this school. All I can tell you is – he moved up here with his mother. They live in the old Collins place."

I decided that my line of questioning had gone well. Preferring not to press my luck, I said, "Well, I won't keep you two. I'm sure you both want to go home."

"Oh no," Mrs Eddy responded, "We've got a couple of activities to organise before even thinking about that."

I smiled at the two teachers and nodded. "I'd better not keep you then. Thanks for the chat."

They moved away and as I was rummaging in my handbag for my car keys I overheard something that gave me food for thought.

Mandy said, "I wonder what she's digging for?"

Mrs Eddy replied, "Well, if it involves the Hoganhoffers, she'd better watch her step."

Roxy and Josh are mesmerised, but I could see Kate needed a spell. I was right. She asked to use my bathroom.

"Sure Kate," I said. "It's just out that door and next to the laundry."

Looking at Roxy and Josh, I tell them, "Okay guys, we're in sight of the finishing line. I'll continue where Kate left off. The end of the story starts now."

One afternoon, while riding my bike home from school, I turned into our street and heard a shout.

I turned around and spotted Kurt pedalling madly in my direction. I stopped and waited for him to catch up. "What's the matter Kurt?

He got off his bike, panting. "There's no problem as long as you keep your trap shut. There's this lawyer bird; she's sniffing around for stuff about Scooter."

Staring at Kurt, I wondered why he was coming on so strong.

I asked, "What for?"

Kurt shrugged. "How would I know? Maybe that stupid, old woman he stayed with knows something.

"If that lawyer bird comes to see you, remember I saved your arse. As a Blood Brother, you owe it to Scooter. Anyway, it's too late to change anything, because if you say something you'll be in big trouble – they call it perjury. They can lock you up and throw away the key. Got it?"

I asked him, "Why are you so full-on about protecting Scooter when you treated him like crap?"

Kurt's face turned bright red with an angry look in his eyes. He puffed out his chest. "Do want to make something of it?"

This time I saw red too and said what I should've said ages ago.

"Nah, Kurt. Just rack off, will ya.

"Every time I see you, you're telling me what to do. I've had it. But I'll keep your dirty little secret, so long as you don't bother me again, right?"

I got back on my bike and peddled off, leaving him standing there. I felt really good inside for the first time in ages, finally telling him exactly what I thought. But that feeling didn't last long.

Riding into our driveway, I noticed a car parked out the front of our house. A woman was sitting in it. She got out of her car puffing on a cigarette. I got off my bike and unhooking my backpack.

My heart started pumping hard because I knew what was coming next.

She walked up the drive and said, "Hi. I'm Kate, is your name Peter?"

"Yes lady," I replied, trying to stay cool.

Then Kate said, "Earlier I was talking to Kurt Hoganhoffer about your friend Scooter, and he said you guys were friends, or rather, Blood Brothers, as he put it."

I tried to put her off. "I don't think I can help you, lady. My Mum and me were out of town when Scooter was found. Kurt knows more than I do. He found him, you know."

Kate smiled, "Yes, I know that. But please call me Kate, because *lady* makes me feel ancient."

I apologised and she said, "How long have you known Scooter and Kurt?"

I tried to give as little away as possible. "Not long really. We only moved up here a short while ago."

Kate could tell I was stalling and tried a different approach.

"Kurt said he didn't know why Scooter hanged himself, but you might know. That's why I'm here."

I looked at her blankly and shook my head. "No. Kurt wouldn't have said that."

"Well Pete, Kurt told me lots of things."

I folded my arms defensively. "Like what?"

Kate smiled. "He told me about how he saved your life. How he watched you from the bush. He saw you change into your swimmers and bounced a rock at you, making you fall in the water. He laughed when I suggested he likes stirring people up. He said it spices things up."

I was stunned. Here was Kurt telling me to keep my trap shut while he was boasting about how he saved me, when it was his fault I fell from the ledge.

What I was thinking must have shown on my face, because Kate quite firmly said, "Peter, I know there's more to Scooter's death than what came out at the Coroner's Inquest.

"None of it adds up with what people have said about Scooter. The truth will come out eventually, so if you know anything please tell me. I'm not asking you to do it now. Just think about it. Here's my card. You can call me anytime during working hours."

Kate stubbed out her cigarette with the toe of her shoe and looked me squarely in the eyes. "Thanks for the chat."

With that, she turned, got into her car and drove off.

As I watched her leave, I felt as if the whole sky had fallen in.

I was trapped. I had nowhere to turn. If I said anything about us being at the swimming hole on the day Rachel was attacked, I could end up in the 'Slammer' with Donny.

Knowing Kurt and his mega-rich Dad, they'd find a way to pin any blame on me. But I was dirty on Kurt causing me to nearly drown, then big-noting himself about saving me and conning me into the Blood Brother bullshit.
It was his fault I'd got caught up in the whole messy business and I didn't know how I could get out of it.

Kurt was just a loser, I decided. I should never have fallen in with him.

Josh and Roxy are listening intently. Roxy puts up her hand up as if she's in class. "If Kurt was such a big loser, why didn't you just tell Kate that you guys were there?"

"Because I didn't know who was responsible. All I knew was, it wasn't me. But hey, who was going to believe me, after all the lies? They might've thought I was involved, eh?"

Kate comes back into the room and asks if she's missed anything.

Josh, who has been very quiet, says, "No, but we heard how you put the heat on our Big Cuz."

"Well, Josh, funny you should say that because the heat is about to be turned up higher. Pete, do you want me to continue, or do you have more to add?"

"No, Kate. You keep going."

Right, let's see. Oh yes, soon after meeting Pete, I received a phone call from Rachel saying she'd remembered something.

I told her to wait for me at her house and I would pick her up in my car. When I arrived at the Pastor's house, Rachel was standing out the front waiting.

As I was about to park, Rachel ran down the path and jumped into the passenger seat. "Hi Kate, you didn't take long to get here."

"I was just on my way out when you called."

Rachel looked at me, "I'm sorry if I stopped you from going some-where."

I laughed. "No. There isn't a problem. You sounded excited over the phone, so I had to come straight away."

Rachel shifted in the seat to face me. "Well, you know when you said if there is anything I'd remembered that didn't come out in court, I should let you know. There is something that came back to me. I don't know why I didn't remember it before. But I think it was because I was in shock straight after. When the court case began, it was even harder to remember stuff. Saying stuff in front of all those people, it was so embarrassing and I felt ashamed."

I patted her arm. "That's alright, Rachel. You don't have to explain. Not to me or anyone else."

Rachel nodded. "Can we go for a ride around the block?"

I looked in the rear-view mirror and said, "Sure."

Rachel closed her eyes and said, "I'm like lying on my bed with my eyes closed not thinking of anything. Then this picture flashes through my mind. When the shirt covered my head, I couldn't see much. But during the struggle, I saw… I… I don't know how to say this, it's embarrassing. I saw his *thing*."

She opened her eyes and looked at me. I wondered if it was to see if I was shocked. But it takes a lot to shock me.

"Rachel, I know it's awkward for you, but can you tell me: what colour was his penis?"

She laughed nervously. "Do you mean if it was Donny's?"

I raised my hand. "No. Just tell me what you saw, please."

Rachel screwed up her face. "I couldn't tell what colour it was. All I remember seeing was his thing and it had a big black mole on it."

I looked out the driver's-side window as I turned left. How mundane to be driving and hearing this crucial information, I thought.

"Well Rachel," I said, "I understand why you didn't want to remember. I also understand how you felt in court.

"Do you realise that if Donny doesn't have a mole, then you might have to give evidence again. How would you feel about that?"

Rachel put both hands up to her mouth. "Kate, I hate the thought of it, but if Donny shouldn't be in prison, I'd have to find a way."

I patted her on the shoulder. "Good girl! I'll drop you home. But please don't tell anyone what you've told me."

Rachel looked shocked. "Are you kidding? It was hard enough telling you that."

Turning back into her street I say, "Rachel, just so you know. That evidence might not be enough to get Donny out of jail. I need some other evidence to tie in the person responsible. I mean, let's face it; we can't exactly get all the guys in town to drop their pants, can we?"

Rachel laughed. "I can't believe you said that."

I laughed too! "Now that would start the tongues wagging, wouldn't it?"

"Wouldn't it ever," Rachel said as we pulled up in her driveway. "Thanks for the ride. See you later." With that, she stepped out of the car.

I reached over and wound down the window so I could say, "It's me who should be doing the thanking. You've handed me the lead I need. I'll be in Brisbane on business tomorrow so my first stop will be to visit Donny."

The next day I drove down to Brisbane and called in at Boggo Road Gaol, having arranged for the special visit the night before.

Donny was over the moon to see me. He stood up and shook my hand with both of his hands, in the same manner as Pastor Carey.

We sat down and he stared straight at me, desperate for some sign that I had good news for him.

"Donny, I've come back to see how you are doing, and I need to ask you one question."

Donny's eyes reflected deep sadness. He waved his hand around, a move I thought must be his way of referring to the prison. He mopped his forehead and flicked his hand as if clearing sweat.

I nodded. "Yes, I know, Donny; it's hard work being here. Even I hate coming here."

Donny banged his fists hard on top of his head. He then tilted his head, resting the side of his face in his hands.

"Are you saying the worst time is at night, trying to sleep?" Donny nodded slowly and turned his thumbs down.

I took a deep breath as I summoned up the courage to have the all-important discussion.

"Well, Donny, I'm going to ask you a funny question. Depending on how you answer, I may be able to help you."

Donny stared at me quizzically for a few moments, then squinted his eyes. He must have been trying to work out what I was leading up to.

Mouthing my words slowly, I said, "Read my lips very, very carefully. It's important. What I want to know is, do you have a black mole on your penis?"

Donny blinked several times. His eyes widened. I wondered if he thought he'd read my lips wrong.

After a few moments, he responded by pointing at himself and then at his groin. He wiggled his little finger.

I confirmed, "Yes, you've understood the question correctly."

Donny put his index finger up to his ear, moved it in little circles and pointed at me.

I laughed. "Yes, you think I'm crazy. But I need to know. It may be important. Do you or don't you have a mole down there?"

Donny shook his head 'no' and stood up. He started pulling down his prison track pants. I jumped to my feet and put my hand up for him to halt. I said, "No. Don't do that, Donny, the guards will take you away. I'll ask one of them to tell me, is that okay?"

Donny wiggled his little finger again and changed his stance to that of a shy child trying to hide.

"Donny, I know it's embarrassing. But it's for the best. Please trust me."

I walked over to one of the prison guards and when I asked him to check Donny's privates for me, he said, not surprisingly, "Hey Miss, you got to be kidding me. You want me to do what? You're saying you want me to look at this prisoner's Whizzer? Is this some sort of joke?"

"I'm sorry, it's no joke," I said. "I'm a lawyer with the Community Advocates Centre and I have some evidence that affects this prisoner's future."

The guard nodded, "Yes, and I suppose the evidence is attached to his Whizzer?"

I smiled. "That's what I'm asking you to verify. I need to know if he has a mole on his Whizzer, as you put it. Yes, or no."

The guard strode over to Donny. "Well, come on then," he said, gesturing for Donny to turn around and pull his track pants down.

The guard had a silly smirk on his face as he moved awkwardly in front of Donny, without making any eye contact.

He looked over Donny's shoulder to me, shook his head 'no', and laughed. "Sure you don't want me to measure it as well?"

I smiled. "That'd be too much information."

The prison guard gestured for Donny to hitch up his pants and remarked, "You got that right, Miss. That little task wasn't in my job description, either."

Those were awkward minutes for all of us. I could only shake the guard's hand and say, "Thank you. You've gone over and above your call of duty, but what you've done might be enough to get this young man out of here. It's very much appreciated."

The guard shrugged and returned to his post.

I gestured for Donny to sit. I did the same.

Looking straight into Donny's eyes, I said, "Donny, I now know you did not touch Rachel."

Donny's eyes lit up. He put the palms of his hands together as if in prayer and raised his eyes to the heavens.
I reached over, took both his hands in mine, and looked earnestly into his eyes. It was imperative to get my message across accurately.

"Hang on, Donny. This is only the first step. I can't guarantee to get you out just yet." Donny closed his eyes tightly and shrugged. I let go of his hands. He pressed his palms together again. I had to tap his hand to get his attention.

He opened his eyes, and I slowly mouthed the words, "Donny, look at me. I need more evidence to appeal your sentence. I may be able to start an application on the basis that you didn't have an interpreter at the trial and didn't understand the proceedings.

"This one piece of information alone is not enough. I have more leads I must follow up. Okay, Donny?"

He nodded enthusiastically and reached out with both his hands to shake mine. With tears in his eyes, he gave me the thumbs-up.

I said, "Donny, trust me. I'm going to do all I can to get you out. But it's going to take time."

Donny's child-like pleading manner got to me. I teared up too. Leaving the Visitors room, I could only think about all he'd gone through.

My next step would be to front up at Pete's place when Pete's mother was home, because I wanted to get to the truth of the boys' differing stories.

By this time Roxy and Josh have realised the gravity of the case. Their 'Big Cuz' was once involved in a serious crime investigation.

Kate sees how focused they are. "I'm sure Pete hasn't forgotten my second visit," she says to both of them.

"Yeah, when Kate showed up, I was like, what story? At that stage, I hadn't told her anything, nor had Kurt. Except about how we first met."

Kate eyeballs me and says, "Remember, I knew you were acting evasive, so I said straight out, I know you and Kurt are hiding some thing. Kurt got to you before we met. You weren't surprised when I turned up at your house."

"That's right, Kate. And I also remember the shock I felt when you said, is your Mum at home? You don't have to answer any of my questions without your parent present – it is that serious."

Kate sits up in her chair and recalls, "You told me, 'She's working and why does she have to be here? I've got nothing to worry about'."

"Then I said to you, well Peter, I hope you're right. Can we go inside? Because I have evidence that Donny didn't assault Rachel. I'm so sure that I'm in the process of preparing an application for an appeal."

"When Kate came out with that, I was thinking, my God, if it wasn't Donny, it must've been Scooter. After all, he was peeping on the teacher. No wonder he couldn't face things.

"Then I realised, bloody hell, maybe this Kate person thinks it's me. I remember blurting out: I know nothing about the Rachel thing."

"Yes," said Kate. "But you were there that day, weren't you?"

Roxy and Josh are listening intently, as Kate and I go back and forth with what happened at our second meeting.

Kate, you had me cornered that day, and I was trying to defend myself.

I said: "Kurt started it. He told Scooter and me to hide and watch out for who might come along. When we saw Donny, he told Scooter to go and pinch Donny's clothes. Then, just as Scooter grabbed Donny's shirt, Kurt chucked this rock into the water, next to Donny.

"Donny came steaming out of the water. We all bolted and that's the God damn truth, lady."

Kate pressed on with her questioning. "If it wasn't you, Peter. Who do you think assaulted Rachel?"

I said, "It must've been Scooter. He had Donny's shirt and, I dunno, he was sort of, into sexual stuff. He had a stack of Nudie books and proudly showed them off to everyone.

"At school one day, he deliberately fell over next to a teacher to look up her dress and told Kurt the colour of her undies. And then there's Scooter's secret. When we became Blood Brothers, we had to give up a secret about ourselves that nobody else knew."

Curled up on the couch, Roxy and Josh are all ears. It's time for me to tell them what happened when we did the 'secrets' part of the Blood Brothers ceremony.

Chapter 7
The Secrets Are Out

Scooter was excited. He wanted to be first to tell his secret.

He closed both hands, put them up to his eyes like binoculars and said, "I spied on the teacher, Miss White. I looked through her bedroom window while she was undressing. I got all excited and went around the back of her house and stole her lace undies off her clothesline."

After Scooter blurted out his secret, Kurt laughed, grabbed him in a bear hug from behind and said, "You're a real Peeping Tom, aren't ya. What are ya?"

Scooter was upset and struggled to get free. He shouted, "Let me go. I'm not a Peeping Tom. I'm Sergeant Schulz."

Kurt let him go. Then he pointed at me. "Yeah, okay. We have to come up with a name for Pete."

Scooter waved both hands in Kurt's face. "But he has to say his secret, first."

Kurt grabbed Scooter's arms, looked at me and said, "Yeah. Scooter's right, come on Pete, out with it. What's your secret?"

I was struggling to think of anything. As I told you all earlier, the only wicked thing I'd done was pinch a few lollies from a Deli. Feeling guilty, I'd chucked them away. I knew Kurt would say it was too weak to qualify as a Blood Brother secret. Then I had a brainstorm.

A few weeks earlier at school, all of the boys were paraded in front of the female toilets and asked to own up to some graffiti. Of course, no one did.

So I said, "Remember the day Principal Kelly hauled all of the guys out of class? Well, it was me: I wrote *Mary Roudle loves to play with Principal Kelly's noodle*."

Kurt had a big smile on his face and chuckled, "So we have one poet and one perve."

You can imagine I was horrified that I had to tell Kate our secrets. And worse, she made me tell her Kurt's secret.

She asked, "Well, is there anything else you haven't told me?"

"Yeah, there is – about Scooter. Kurt told me he found a note next to where Scooter… ahh… did… you know."

Kate's face was deadpan, but I noticed that she flinched ever so slightly. She'd heard something significant in my words.

She came back at me with: "Oh, did he, now?

"Well, Pete, what if I told you that Scooter could barely write his own name, let alone construct a sentence?

What do you think about Kurt and his secret, now?"

I was puzzled. I realised if Kurt had lied about the note, he might have told other lies. I felt as if a bomb had been dropped on me.

Kate waited a moment or two before saying, "I know it's a big shock. So, what are you thinking?"

Well, after I heard that information, I was thinking: Scooter's dead. Donny's in prison. My life's been hell since it all happened. Then there's Rachel – what must she have gone through? And I'm, like, protecting the guy that did it. God, I can't believe I didn't get it.

Kurt had used me, like he used Scooter. God damn it! Not anymore! He had been so smug about his secret. It was a shocker.

"Great!" Roxy shouts. "Hurry up, Uncle Pete, I like secrets. What was

Kurt's secret? Why was it shocking?"

"Okay Roxy, let me get on with the story."

I decided to tell Kate exactly what Kurt revealed at the Blood Brother ceremony.

When it came to his turn, he'd laughed and said, "Looks like we have three 'P's' for our secrets." At the same time, he dropped his shorts and showed us a big black mole on his penis.

I'd never seen anything like it before. Aside from showing off his mole, I was stunned by the way he'd just flopped his private bits out for all to see. He seemed proud of that mole.

Scooter was giggling like it was some kind of taboo. Flapping his hands, he began chanting: "I know nothzing, I see nothzing, I say nothzing."

When I finished reliving this event, Kate stood up, patted me on the shoulder and said, "Thank you Peter, for being so forthright.

"I have enough evidence now to put Kurt away. It's important information and if you'd come forward with it earlier, you would have saved everyone a lot of trouble."

She wasn't pulling any punches; I felt a bit scared.

"Yes, I know," I said. "So what happens now?"

"Well, that's up to you, Peter. First thing I'd do if I were you is to tell your Mum. I assume she doesn't know anything about this."

That was true. "Oh jeez," I said. "She's going to go ballistic when she finds out."

Kate came back into the storytelling again.

Yes, Pete and I told you, "Isn't it better coming from you, rather than someone else?"

Before I left, I said, "The next thing will be that I'll get you to sign a sworn statement about what happened on that day of the Blood Brother ceremony, what happened with Donny and his shirt, and the other things we've talked about. Then you might have to appear in court as one of my star witnesses."

You asked me, "What about Kurt? What are you going to do about him?"

I told you to leave Kurt to me. I'd be going to the dairy to talk with him and his father. Judging by his father's reputation, I expected that to be difficult.

You were worried. You didn't think Kurt and his Dad would even let me on the premises. What's more, you believed the Hoganhoffers could protect themselves with their wealth.

I said, "Pete, I'll give you a tip. All of Daddy's money is not going to get Kurt out of trouble this time."

After my talk with Kurt and his father, I'll be going to the police and making a statement.

Pete, you looked so worried; I think you were cross with yourself for buying into the pathetic Blood Brother pact and as a result keeping secrets.

Josh asked, "So, Cuz, what did Aunty Dawn say when she found out what was going on and why Kate was there?"

"Josh, Mum was surprisingly calm about it. She said she'd known for a while that something wasn't right with me. I'd become moody. She'd asked me a few times if everything was going okay at school, but I'd just said 'yes' and clammed up.

"Mum put my attitude down to how Scooter had died. She said she hoped I'd learnt something from what had happened, and that she was glad I wasn't involved. She told me to be more careful about the friends I made in future. Ring any bells for you, Josh?"

Roxy butts in. "Yeah, Josh. Big alarm bells. DING! DING! DING!"

Josh pokes his tongue out, "What would you know?"

"Hey, you two, cut that out! I'll stop the story right now if you keep that up."

They quiet down and settle back into the couch to listen.

Giving them a warning glance, I say, "Right Kate, sorry about the rude interruption, please continue."

"Okay, thanks Pete. So, we start again at the Hoganhoffers."

The dairy visit went as I expected.

It was late afternoon when I arrived, just after a shower of rain. I drove through the gate just as the sun came out. Noticing a rainbow standing proudly in a bright green paddock, I took it as a sign of truth or justice to come.

I pulled up near the house and got out. A barking cattle dog greeted me. I heard a voice scolding the dog and spotted Kurt up on the porch. Taking a deep breath, I marched up to the steps, the dog sniffing around my ankles.

Kurt said, "Sorry lady, about the dog. He won't bite."

I stared straight into Kurt's blue eyes and asked, "Do you remember me from the other day?"

Kurt was quick to avert his eyes, "Yeah, that's right, you're Kate. Come for a look around the dairy, have you?"

"No. I've come to talk to you and Mr Hoganhoffer if he's home."

Kurt moved down a step towards me, "Why do you want my Dad here?"

"There are some questions I'm going to ask you and I think he should be here when you answer them."

Kurt folded his arms defensively and said, "I've got nothing to hide. So what's the big deal?"

I was getting impatient with his smart tone of voice and replied, "Is your father here or not?"

Kurt was also annoyed, "No! He's in town at the Shire offices."

"Well Kurt, if I were you, I'd ring him right now. Because I don't want to be accused of pressuring you into saying something you might regret."

Kurt's face became taut. Through clenched teeth, he said, "Doesn't matter to me what you say. I've done nothing. It will be you that'll regret coming here because my Dad doesn't like being interrupted when he's on business."

I marched down the steps and said, "That's fine by me. I'll wait for him in the car."

I walked back to the car and with my nerves starting to get to me, I lit up a cigarette.

Kurt watched me for a few minutes before retreating into the house.

I'd puffed my way through two more before a black Mercedes came gliding up the driveway.

A short, balding, grim-faced man wearing a dark suit walked past my car and up the front steps. The front door opened, and Kurt pointed in my direction, shrugging his shoulders.

I stubbed out my cigarette, got out of my car and met Kurt's father halfway between the steps and my car.

I held out my hand and said, "Hello Mr HoganHoffer. I'm Kate Maybury and I am with the Community Advocates Centre.
I'm acting for Donny Buckle in his appeal against his conviction."

Mr Hoganhoffer ignored my offer of a handshake. He was angry. "What's this got to do with me or Kurt?"

"There is evidence that Kurt and two other boys were at Hanging Tree Gorge on the day Rachel Carey was assaulted and I just want to ask Kurt a couple of questions. I thought it best for you to be here."

Mr Hoganhoffer turned around and shouted, "Kurt! Come here right now and answer this lady's questions."

He turned his attention back to me and said, "I'm sure it's all a mistake."

Kurt was very reluctant to join us and stood by the door.

Mr Hoganhoffer called out again, "Kurt! Come here right now and don't waste my time. I have important business to finish."

Kurt slowly shuffled down the stairs towards us and onto the driveway.

His hands were in his jean's pockets. He stood facing the sun and pulled a hand out, shading his face to avoid eye contact.

I said, "Kurt, I want you to listen carefully. I know that you, Peter Gannon and Scooter were at the Gorge on the day that Rachel Carey was assaulted."

Kurt's confident manner gave way to stumbling words, "Lady, I... ahh didn't do anything. The court... err umm said it was Donny. Whatever Pete said to you... ahh... he's lying."

I had him on the run. Time to take a softer approach, I decided.

"You could be right, Kurt. That's why I need your version of events.

"You say Pete's lying? Well, Pete says you told him Scooter left a suicide note. Is that true?"

Kurt paused for a moment. I think he was trying to figure out what not to say and replied, "No. He's not lying about that.

"When I found Scooter, he... he left a note saying that he was sorry for... for what he done. I didn't know it was the girl. After what happened, I... I threw it away so he wouldn't get into trouble."

I looked squarely into Kurt's baby-blue eyes and said, "So it's true? You were all there the day Rachel Carey was assaulted?"

Kurt looked away and then at the ground. "Yeah. But I was only protecting Scooter. I... I didn't know things would end up this way."

I said, "Okay, that's all I need for now."

Kurt seems surprised. "Is that it?"

I turned to Mr Hoganhoffer. "Well, that's it for now. The police will be in touch to get a statement from Kurt, so thank you for your time."

As I walked away, under my breath, I mouthed the words: "Gotcha, you lying bastard. Now I have all the evidence I need."

I felt like turning cartwheels down that driveway!

Of course, this was far from the end of things. We had to lodge an appeal and ask the court for Donny to be released on compassionate grounds, based on the new evidence.

"What happened to that arsehole, Kurt," Josh asks Kate.

"Okay, Josh, here's how it all went down."

Kurt was charged: that set off a chain-reaction. Firstly, the local paper, the Pomona Post, tried to question the motive of the Police in charging Kurt. The article argued Donny had a fair trial and was found guilty. It glossed over the truth to convince its readers that justice had been served.

I suspect the paper had a close relationship with Mr Hoganhoffer.

I jump in to back Kate on that.

Yeah, Kate's right. All hell let loose. The article divided the town. Both sides had their prejudices, which had nothing to do with justice – or who was guilty.

Some townsfolk saw the Hoganhoffers as Pomona's financial lifeline. Such a scandal could threaten their livelihoods and donations. Others didn't like Mr Hoganhoffer's influence and the power he wielded.

Then, a small but highly vocal group led by Pastor Carey launched a campaign demanding Donny's release. That resulted in a petition being presented to the Solicitor General's Office."

"Jeez," exclaims Josh. "Since Kurt did it, I wouldn't have thought the case would cause that much trouble. It's getting bigger than Ben Hur!"

I can tell it's dawning on Josh that this is not a story; it's a series of life-changing events.

Choosing my words carefully, I tell him:

"Now you see, Josh, how one small decision can change everything and create a much bigger problem. Once the Genie is out of the bottle, there is no going back.

Pressure mounted on Kate too, as to her motives. The newspaper tried to cast doubt on her credentials. It even questioned why she'd left the big legal firm in Brisbane and moved to a backwater town. It was a flaky article at best, and the bastards didn't name who provided the information about Kate. They just mentioned *'from an unnamed source'*.

Kate picks up her glass and goes into the kitchen for some water.

As she comes back in, she comments, "I never expected that kind of backlash, when all I was doing was getting to the truth. Yet others who had sparse knowledge of the case seemed to think they had a better idea of the truth than I did."

Josh asks, "How did you handle that?"

Kate sits down and tells him: "More hard work followed, Josh. Here's what we did."

With help from a handful of volunteers, we raised some funds and put together an appeal to the court. It was supported by Pastor Carey's petition.

The small group who'd organised the petition came with me to the Supreme Court. We presented an urgent application to the Attorney General for Donny to be released, pending a judicial review and invited the Press to be present when we attended the court.

The Attorney General agreed to release Donny if the Court of Appeal's application to apply for leave to appeal was granted.

And the appeal was granted.

Pastor Carey and I went to Boggo Road Gaol for Donny's release.

When we arrived, TV cameras and the Press reporters were waiting for us outside the prison gates. There was also a group of Indigenous people protesting about Aboriginal justice. They had big banners and some Aboriginal Land Rights flags.

Kate puts down her glass of water and pauses. "It was mayhem: we had to run the gauntlet through the TV cameras and the reporters.

Once inside, we made our way to the Administration centre to meet Donny and the prison Superintendent.

When he saw us, Donny's face lit up with the biggest grin. I wanted to burst into tears, seeing his joy and relief. He jumped up from his chair, gave me a massive hug and stepped back. He pointed to himself and circled the fingers of one hand around his ear.

I said, "Yes, I know. You're going crazy in here." Donny turned to Pastor Carey, shaded his eyes with this left hand and bowed his head.

Pastor Carey took Donny's right hand in a handshake. "Donny, no! You have no need to feel guilty about anything," the Pastor said. "It's we who should feel guilty; those of us who let you down and didn't believe you."

I notice Kate becoming emotional as she relives this scene.

"So Josh," she says, "that was a big moment in my life and more was to come. Let me continue."

The day of Donny's release on appeal was joyous. I watched his reactions closely. He looked at me and with tears in his eyes he placed one hand over his heart. He then intertwined his fingers on both hands, as if praying and shook them up and down.

I asked him, you mean in your heart you didn't think you would be free, yet you prayed it would happen?

He nodded, smiled, and gave the thumbs-up sign.

The Superintendent handed Donny a release form. Donny had to make his mark on this form to retrieve his meagre belongings and some cash saved from prison work.

Donny waved the banknotes and smiled. He moved his hands around in a circle and pretended he had a knife and fork, cutting something."

I had to smile. "Excuse me, Donny. Are you saying you want to spend your money on a good meal?"

Donny gave us the thumbs-up and stuck out his thumb and little finger as if they were horns.

"Right," I said. "You want a nice juicy steak dinner."

Donny nodded 'yes' enthusiastically. Donny may have been hungry, but he wasn't as hungry as the 'news hounds' waiting to ambush him outside the prison.

To help us avoid them, the prison's Superintendent had arranged for a vehicle to take us out through another exit.

It wasn't a clean get-away because some reporters were wise to this and spotted us leaving the alternate exit. They chased us, banging on the car to get a 'photo op' reaction.

Donny was wide-eyed with shock. I explained to him that everyone was interested in his story. His shook his hands and head 'no'.

He made it clear he did not want publicity, nor did he want compensation money. All he wanted was for everyone to know he was innocent. He was not a criminal: he hadn't touched or harmed Rachel in any way.

I look at my young cousins and see that Josh is deep in thought. Realising this is not quite the end of the story, he asks:

"After Donny was set free what happened with his appeal?"

Kate stands up to stretch her back. "Well, we ploughed on. It had to be a neat and tidy wrap up for Donny. There were still many more steps to the finish line. This is what we had to do next."

Donny had indicated strongly he wanted only to have the conviction overturned and was not interested in money. As it was reasonable to expect compensation, we applied for it.

The Court of Appeal granted his release based on new evidence. However, the court did not agree to any compensation because it ruled the trial judge and jury had not erred in their decision, despite Donny not having an interpreter. Their reasoning was based on the evidence available at the time: the jury reached the right verdict and there was no misdirection by the judge.

Kate takes a few sips of the water while I explain to Roxy and Josh that the Court of Appeal takes this stance to defend itself – the justice system – from criticism.

Mounting pressure was put on the Government to make an ex-gratia payment to Donny's trustee to help him re-settle elsewhere. This meant Donny would be leaving his home with Pastor Carey's family, and Pomona.

The Coroner's Inquest into Scooter's death was re-opened. It could not be proved that Kurt had anything to do with his suicide, but I reckon he would have hounded Scooter if Donny have gotten off.

Did Kurt expect Scooter to 'top' himself? Maybe, maybe not.

Josh asks: "What happened to that rotten arsehole?"

Kate arches her aching back again as she responds, "Fortunately, faced with the damning evidence against him, Kurt pleaded guilty to the charges: he admitted to raping Rachel.

He at least saved Pete and Rachel from having to testify. He got five years in Juvenile Detention and was eligible for parole in three years."

Roxy stands up. She stretches and sighs, "Wow, that was some story Big Cuz, but where's Donny now? I like him."

"Well, after what had happened, the Carey family felt they couldn't have him back. He had to relocate; leave Pomona.

Pastor and Mrs Carey found a foster family on a farm out west to take him. It turns out it is the same pastoral station where he was born.

Last I heard, he was happy – working cattle like a top Jackaroo. Cattle don't discriminate or make judgements, like people do.

He reconnected with his tribe, the Runga-Rungawah. They look on him as a hero, because of the injustice he conquered despite the problems he faced.

Roxy said, "Wow, I'm glad it worked out for him. And what about that Rachel chick?"

"I can answer that," says Kate. "We still keep in touch from time to time. She went to Uni and did fashion design along with some part-time modelling. She's still in the fashion industry and owns a boutique in Melbourne."

I see that Josh is staring blankly into space. I guess he's got a lot on his mind right now.

Bringing him back to the present, I say, "Hey matey, you're miles away."

Josh shakes his head. "Yeah, it all makes you think. It all got so complicated."

Time to hit him with the all-important question:

"Josh, do you think you are man enough to make the right decision for yourself? You know, I wasn't man enough to speak up when I should've."

"I'm not sure right now. I'll have to think about it very hard."

Kate looks at Josh, "Whatever you decide, go with your gut feeling, not your head, and make a decision that is right for you – not anyone else."

Roxy is curious. "What decision, Josh?"

"You keep your nose out. This is secret men's business. Not for nosey sister," he replies.

I intervene before senseless bickering can start. At the same time, Aunt Barbara has turned into my driveway. "Okay, okay that's enough from you two. Just as well your Mum's pulling in the drive."

I usher them out and say, "Thanks for coming over and thanks for the excellent T-shirt."

They wave to Kate and shout together, "See ya Kate, see ya, Big Cuz," then run down the drive and jump into their Mum's car.

I turn to Kate and say, "I reckon we wore them out." We go back inside and sit down. I think to myself, I'm worn out too. Re-telling the story has reminded me how scared I was when events began to unfold.

I remark to Kate, "Boy, it brings those times back into sharp focus, eh. There are bits of the story I wasn't aware of until you filled them in."

"Yes, it does. What a life-changing event for all of us. Meeting Donny and Rachel, and the sadness of Scooter's short life touched me deeply.

"I learnt a lot: my tough edge softened. After vowing in early life I'd never marry, never have children, here I am with a gorgeous Hubby and a son.

"What about you, Pete? How do you think it changed you?"

"For me, it wasn't that dramatic. I picked my friends more carefully after. I became less trusting. People had to earn my trust. From then on, I was careful to make sure any holes I dug I could see out of them."

Kate stands and stretches. "Yes, it's a valuable life lesson we all had, that's for sure.

"Now, Pete, I'm heading home. It was great to catch up and go over old times. I hope we helped Josh – and Roxy too."

Kate gives me a warm hug. I see her out and watch from the verandah as she drives away into the night.

I'm thinking there weren't any winners in our story, except maybe the universe, after the Karma worked through.

My concern is for young Josh. I have to trust that he's now armed with more awareness, and he'll make the right decision.

Dob in a mate? He might have to do just that.

Each of us had a cross to bear.

I start to daydream. I'm picturing myself on my surfboard looking out for that perfect wave, so I'm ready for it when it comes.

Calmness falls over me as I ride the wave of my thoughts. Surfing is like the universe – everything goes in cycles. I reckon it, too, strives for perfection.

Why do I say that? Well. I have this feeling that the 'stuff' of life goes around full circle until it's fixed. Justice was tested at Pomona and most wrongs put right.

A voice inside me says, but hey, what about Scooter? Where's the justice in it for him?

Believing in past existences, I have this vision of Scooter in a past life being the accuser of Darby, the black tracker, who was hanged for a crime he did not commit. Donny may have been Darby. As for the rest of us, well, perhaps we were the mob that did the lynching. While Kurt was the one who stole the cows and allowed an innocent man to die at the end of a rope.

Re-telling the story has shown me order has been restored – a cycle completed after nearly one hundred years.

I just realised, even Donny got to return to his roots and be with his people. Is that fanciful? Perhaps, but it is strange, almost eerie, how history repeated itself at Pomona.

One thing's for sure: Kurt was an absolute control freak. Always out to shock and be the centre of attention. His manipulations were designed to disturb the lives of others. He obviously didn't pay any attention to the Bible saying, *whatsoever a man soweth, that shall he also reap.*

The irony is that as a result of Kurt's need to control, he's gone into a situation where he has no control at all. He's being told when to eat and when to shit.

Is it possible to feel sorry for such a person? Yes and no.

Kurt had everything he could ever want, but perhaps not what he needed most. I can only guess at what was missing from his life with his parents.

Well, the scandal Kurt caused, drastically changed his parents lives too. Old Hoganhoffer chucked his wife out and sold up everything. According to rumours, he moved overseas – far away as possible I'd reckon, eh?

I go back inside. I yawn loudly as I flop down into *old faithful.*

Soon I start to nod off, but my thoughts are crystal clear. I see how the events Kurt created, hurt many people.

For me, it was as if I'd been 'dancing in the dark'. Firstly, you don't know who you're dancing with.

Secondly, they're trying to lead – you're following, but you don't know where.

Thirdly, you wonder if they're moving to the same steps or same tune as you. Scared that you might stumble and fall, you can only hope the music will stop and the lights will come back on.

You could say the same about life. It's all 'dancing in the dark'. Just ask Donny, eh?

Epilogue

I guess you are wondering what Josh did about his dilemma? I later learnt from him that he didn't 'dob' in his best friend Paul as I expected he would.

I am very proud of him by the decision he took. It turns out he confronted Paul and said that he knew he stole the money and if he didn't return it and own up, Josh would report him to the Principal and they would no longer be friends.

Seems the guilty party took the advice, confessed and returned the money. As punishment Paul agreed to front up and apologise for the distress he caused at the school assembly. It was decided by Brian's family (the accused boy) that no further action would be taken.

Peter Gannon signing off

Remembering the Innocent

In the Preface I refer to the following wrongfully convicted people that inspired this story and cannot end the story without acknowledging those who have been victims of the justice system at the hands of Eric Edgar Cooke, which brought them all together. Their stories and photos are on the blog page of my website:

www.blood-ties-bloody-lies.com.au

Estelle Blackburn – Author

Estelle Blackburn, Investigative Journalist, was instrumental in reviewing evidence that would eventually lead to lodgement of appeals by both John Button and Darryl Beamish. Their convictions were overturned and Estelle published an award winning book: Broken Lives – The Complete Life and Crimes of Serial Killer Eric Edgar Cooke published in 2002 by Hardie Grant, South Yarra, Vic. IBSN: 978-1-74064-073-2

The Late Andrew Mallard

Andrew Mallard was wrongfully convicted in 1995 of the murder of Pamela Lawrence, a Mosman Park Jewellery shop owner. Andrew was sentenced to life imprisonment at the age of 32.

Almost 12 years later, after two Supreme Court appeals and finally an appeal to the High Court, his conviction was quashed and a retrial ordered. Andrew was released from prison in 2006. At the time, the Director of Public Prosecutions stated; "that Mallard remained the prime suspect and that if further evidence became available he may still be prosecuted.

Andrew was paid compensation by the WA state government. Later in 2006, police conducted a 'cold-case' review of the Lawrence murder. As a result, they uncovered sufficient evidence to charge already convicted murderer Simon Rochford with the murder of Pamela Lawrence and eliminate Mallard as a suspect. After being publicly named as the suspect, Rochford committed suicide in Albany Prison.

Tragically, Andrew Mallard's life was ended in April 2019. He was killed by a hit and run driver while crossing Sunset Boulevard in Hollywood, California.

Other notable wrongful murder convictions;

- Lindy Chamberlain and the death of her daughter Azaria.

- Colin Campbell Ross of Melb, executed and exonerated posthumously 1921.

- Edward Splatt of S.A. murder of 77yo Rosa Simper in 1977.

- David Szach of S.A. murder of 44yo lover, Derrance Stevenson 1979.

- Aboriginal Kevin Condren of QLD murder in 1984. Conviction overturned 1990.

- Graham Stafford of QLD murder in of 12yo girl, Leanne Sarah Holland in 1991, released 2006.

- Henry Keogh, S.A., murder of 29yo fiancée, Anna-Jane Cheney in 1994 released after 21 years.

About the Author

Born and raised on the West Coast of Australia, T J Ward has always enjoyed writing. Areas of interest include: all things metaphysical, Alternate Science, studying sacred geometry and researching harmonic theory.

Having written several magazine articles of an esoteric nature and published through New Dawn Magazine and Uncensored Magazine News. T J ventured into writing stories and novels.

In 2018 he released his first Self-Published novel Zero to Hero, which was a natural progression from his previous magazine publications.

Zero to Hero is about an imaginary Sci-Fi world that morphs into reality and how the two young protagonists, Leo and Dani find themselves no longer in control of the game. Facing repercussions and responsibilities beyond their mere teenage years, while never really knowing what or who to trust.

As the world turned and changed T J found himself revisiting a previously penned novella with uncanny and parallel connections to current global events.

Blood Ties Bloody Lies is a fictional tale of injustice set in the not so politically correct era of the late 1970's. By todays standards what we saw as normal and mundane attitudes back then, have now become unjust and abhorrent in themselves.

If this story hits a spot within you, then T J will have succeeded in shedding some light on injustice and how much we still need to evolve.

Visit

www.blood-ties-bloody-lies.com.au
To discover more about this novel
and the Author T J Ward

To find out more about T J's previously
penned articles and Zero to Hero

Visit: www.jameswardpublishing.com